SPECIAL MESSAGE TO READERS

This book is published under the auspices of

THE ULVERSCROFT FOUNDATION

(registered charity No. 264873 UK)

Established in 1972 to provide funds for research, diagnosis and treatment of eye diseases. Examples of contributions made are: —

A Children's Assessment Unit at Moorfield's Hospital, London.

•

Twin operating theatres at the Western Ophthalmic Hospital, London.

•

A Chair of Ophthalmology at the Royal Australian College of Ophthalmologists.

•

The Ulverscroft Children's Eye Unit at the Great Ormond Street Hospital For Sick Children, London.

You can help further the work of the Foundation by making a donation or leaving a legacy. Every contribution, no matter how small, is received with gratitude. Please write for details to:

**THE ULVERSCROFT FOUNDATION,
The Green, Bradgate Road, Anstey,
Leicester LE7 7FU, England.
Telephone: (0116) 236 4325**

**In Australia write to:
THE ULVERSCROFT FOUNDATION,
c/o The Royal Australian College of
Ophthalmologists,
27, Commonwealth Street, Sydney,
N.S.W. 2010.**

Gerald Hammond worked as an architect for thirty years, before taking early retirement in 1982. He lives in Scotland, with his wife, and has three sons and five granddaughters. He spends his time shooting, fishing and writing — 'Anything else I do reluctantly and under protest.'

He is the author of over forty mystery novels. He currently writes three mystery series: one featuring dogbreeder John Cunningham, one based around the gun expert Keith Calder and one set in the world of angling, featuring Walter James.

DEAD WEIGHT

When Jasmine Horner is found drowned, no one is sorry to see the back of her. In fact, there are those who feel that after a lifetime of meddling in other people's business her comeuppance is long overdue. An innocent conversation in the local pub leads the police to Alistair Branch — much to the consternation of his friend, John Cunningham. And when Alistair is arrested John enlists several of his young kennel hands to gather information. Gradually, a series of possible clues is uncovered. And matters finally reach a crescendo when a chance discovery leads to a dramatic confrontation . . .

Books by Gerald Hammond
Published by The House of Ulverscroft:

DEAD GAME
THE REWARD GAME
FAIR GAME
SILVER CITY SCANDAL
THE LOOSE SCREW
MUD IN HIS EYE
COUSIN ONCE REMOVED
SAUCE FOR THE PIGEON
FRED IN SITU
THE WORRIED WIDOW
ADVERSE REPORT
STRAY SHOT
DOG IN THE DARK
DOGHOUSE
A BRACE OF SKEET
WHOSE DOG ARE YOU?
LET US PREY
HOME TO ROOST
STING IN THE TAIL
LAST RIGHTS
THE EXECUTOR
THE GOODS
PURSUIT OF ARMS
FINE TUNE
A SHOCKING AFFAIR

GERALD HAMMOND

DEAD WEIGHT

Complete and Unabridged

ULVERSCROFT
Leicester

First published in Great Britain in 2000 by
Macmillan Publishers Limited
London

First Large Print Edition
published 2001
by arrangement with
Macmillan Publishers Limited
London

British Library CIP Data

Hammond, Gerald, *1926* –
    Dead weight.—Large print ed.—
    Ulverscroft large print series: mystery
    1. Cunningham, John (Fictitious character)
    2. Detective and mystery stories 3. Large type books
    I. Title
    823.9'14 [F]

    ISBN 0–7089–4416–7

Published by
F. A. Thorpe (Publishing)
Anstey, Leicestershire

Set by Words & Graphics Ltd.
Anstey, Leicestershire
Printed and bound in Great Britain by
T. J. International Ltd., Padstow, Cornwall

This book is printed on acid-free paper

1

'You're tired, John,' Beth informed me, looking up from her crouched position among the roses. 'You've done enough. Knock off and go down to the pub. Have a pint of Guinness,' she added. 'You could take Myrtle and Polly with you. Be back by seven.'

In case there is any doubt in the reader's mind, Beth is my wife. Not every wife says that sort of thing but Beth is exceptional, partly because she is always afraid of a relapse into the illness which terminated my army career. She is convinced that Guinness will put back a little much-needed weight onto my bones. It is not a delusion which I am in any hurry to dispel.

I might have put up an argument, but in fact there was very little work left to do. It was the height of summer and the kennels were full, but it was also the school holidays. Over the years, instead of increasing the year-round staff, we had built up a select band of young 'volunteers' who, with the enthusiastic approval of their parents and in return for 'gifts' of pocket money considerably less than the minimum wage, would come in and help with the dog-walking, bathing and grooming, run-cleaning and feeding and even, in selected cases, elementary training. An intelligent, carefully instructed teenager could enjoy instilling the basics of 'Come' and 'Heel' and 'Sit' (or 'Hup') into a spaniel puppy and in the process probably learn as much as his or her charge. More advanced training in hunting and retrieving for our stock of young working spaniels was well in hand. Even the garden was as immaculate as the dogs would permit and Beth's continued gardening was no more than her personal therapy.

I was leg-weary and might have preferred to put my feet up in front of the telly but, as usual in summer, there was nothing on the box that anyone with two brain cells to rub together could possibly want to watch, so I gave Beth a kiss on the less muddy of her two cheeks, gathered Polly and Myrtle (our two best brood bitches) and set off by a path running parallel to, but a safe hundred yards from, the road.

A hot day was giving way to a beautiful evening. The air over north-east Fife was cooling, the light softening. In the middle distance but just within earshot a tractor was gathering the straw bales left by the harvester and rooks were squabbling around a wood on the skyline. Too far overhead to be audible, a jet was drawing a straight line across the sky. It was good to see butterflies making a comeback even if their offspring were less than welcome on our vegetables.

Each of the bitches was already a Field Trial Champion, now retired from active service except for occasional bouts of motherhood, and so tended to be left to last in the routine of walking and training. But young rabbits were bobbing in the hedge-bottoms among a blaze of wildflowers. They both knew better than to give chase, but Myrtle thrust into a bed of ground elder and put up a cock pheasant, a wanderer from one of the several shoots thereabouts. The bird rocketed, clocking indignantly, then set his wings and glided to a strip of gorse bushes fringed by rabbit holes. He might still be around in October but I doubted it. Somebody would snare him before then or bring him to hand by the use of raisins soaked in whisky.

The path brought us to the back door of the pub and we made our way inside. The 'pub' is, in fact, a former coaching inn which has grown rather haphazardly over the years to meet the demand generated by remarkably good cuisine, without ever being subjected to brewer's modernizations beyond the laying of quarry tiles on the floor. Thus the public bar, all white paint and dark woodwork, wanders around some surprising corners and has windows opening onto unexpected views. For much of the day it is a place of quiet calm and we seemed to have caught it at its quietest, between the visits of the opening-time quickies and the arrival of the home-going commuters.

Among the charms of the pub, in my view, were the facts that it was in the village and so was just the right distance from Three Oaks Kennels for a leisurely stroll; and that the proprietors welcomed dogs with the sole proviso that they were house trained and well behaved. They could hardly do otherwise, to the displeasure of hygiene inspectors and the anti-dog brigade, when the Hebdens' own two dogs, a chocolate Labrador named Angus, and Hector, some kind of terrier of uncertain breeding, had the run of the place.

Hector and Angus were well acquainted with Myrtle and Polly, though not as well acquainted as they would have liked at certain seasons, and they made room for them in front of the dead fireplace. The bar seemed otherwise deserted, but Mrs Hebden, who usually did bar duty until the hour when paid bar staff began their shifts, appeared like a genie from a trap to serve my pint of

Guinness and remained dutifully to chat about the weather and the doings of the day. A fat and friendly lady with unnaturally yellow hair, she was a fountain of local gossip more than equalling the *Fife Herald*.

I was not to have my side of the bar to myself for long. Henry Kitts, the elderly husband of Isobel (the third member of the partnership in the kennels) put his creased and raddled face round the door before I had paid for my drink. 'So I've caught up with you,' he said. 'Isobel says she'll walk down and join me here when it's time for you to go home.' Replying to my raised eyebrows, he added, 'A dram and a pint of Eighty Shilling.'

I repeated the order. That is the penalty for being first at the bar. I willed Mrs Hebden to finish up and give me my change before any other thirsty friends arrived (because, as a one-drink man, I found it an expensive folly to become involved in the ritual of 'rounds') but it was not to be. She pottered with the till until Alistair Branch made an appearance and took the stool on the other side of Henry.

Alistair was retired — from being something in insurance, I believed. A stocky man with a thatch of silver hair, he had the unlined face of the truly serene. He looked, in fact, like that rarity — a saint with a sense of humour. At his heel was June (short for

Juniper), a springer bitch who we had sold to Alistair several years earlier after she had provided us with her permitted complement of pups. The two were inseparable, pottering away the years together in desultory pursuit of rabbit and pigeon, and wildfowl in season. Alistair could well have afforded membership of a quality pheasant syndicate but I secretly sympathized with his view that anyone forking out that sort of money for birds of which only a small percentage would be remembered at the end of each day had to have more money than sense. Rough-shooting, he could pursue agricultural pests, summer as well as winter. June came to say hello to her one-time master and shooting companion and then went to join the growing throng at the fireplace.

Alistair was a friend and near-contemporary of Henry's rather than mine, but that did not excuse me from the traditional courtesies. Alistair accepted a large Grouse and Mrs Hebden at last got around to making change. The next arrival could buy his own or take over the chair.

The unusual heatwave could have been expected to take up several minutes of conversation, but Alistair dismissed it in about three words. He was a reserved character, not given to showing emotion, but his usual air of serenity was absent and he gave the impression that there was something needling him. A pull at his whisky did little to improve his mood. 'Who would you say was the rudest man in the village?' he asked suddenly.

The question was not one to be answered lightly. I was turning over several contenders in my mind when Henry nodded towards me and said, 'John, of course.'

'Would you?' I said, surprised. I do not suffer fools gladly and I have what Beth calls a 'cutting edge to my tongue', but I thought that I was seldom rude. 'It seems to me,' I told Henry, 'that you've just put yourself in line for the title. Anyway, there must be somebody ruder than I am — even if I can't think who just for the moment.'

'Me, for instance?' Alistair said.

'You're an also-ran,' Henry told him. 'A novice. A non-starter.' And it was true. Although not quite Henry's age, Alistair gave the impression of being a rather shy, very courteous gentleman of the old school. 'We don't have an actual trophy for the event yet,' Henry went on, 'but I might be persuaded to present one. Who's been suggesting that you're in line for the challenge cup?'

Alistair hesitated, too much the gentleman to bandy a lady's name in the pub. But his grievance was rankling and some names could do with a little bandying. 'Mrs Horner.' I had the impression that only respect for the house restrained him from spitting over his shoulder after uttering the name.

Henry, who had begun to drink his beer, snorted suddenly and had to make use of his handkerchief. 'Look who was talking!' he said. 'The pot calling the kettle black. What did you do? Refuse to lay your coat in a puddle for her to walk over? Or hold up a mirror?'

Almost opposite the pub a minor road (Old Ford Road) ran away into the countryside, serving farms and a sand-pit. Half a dozen houses, rather larger and of better quality than the average for the village, had been built along one side of the road. The other side, ragged with bushes and a few mature trees, fell away steeply to a burn. Mrs Horner, I knew, lived in the first house fronting the road and Alistair, I thought, in the fourth or fifth. 'A clash between neighbours?' I suggested. 'What in Glasgow they'd call a stairheid?'

'Not exactly. It's a long story.' Alistair sighed. 'Same again?'

I had not finished my pint of Guinness and when I finished it I would normally have set off for home. But Mrs Horner, although I hardly knew her, was one of my least favourite people and I would not have wanted to miss anything that reflected unfavourably on her. I accepted a half. Henry, who would also be walking home, took the same again.

'It goes back years,' Alistair said, 'to when we'd just moved into the village. We used to walk June along the road. Well, more particularly, I used to walk her along the road to the pub or the shop. I didn't know that Mrs Horner's feu included some of the rough ground on the other side of the road, or so she says. That was the logical place for June to run around and do her business, but one day Mrs Horner rushed out and accosted me. Honestly, from the way she carried on you'd think that I had personally crapped on her doorstep. You wouldn't believe it.'

'Yes I would,' I said. 'I met her in the street in Cupar one day, and for once I didn't have a dog with me. Without a hello or goodbye and in fewer words than I'd have believed possible, she suggested that the reason I was alone was because no dog would walk with me any more.'

'That sounds about par for the course,' Alistair said. 'When she pointed it out, I saw then that the first twelve inches or so from the road was mown, but I'll swear that June had never messed on that.

'I'm all for the peaceful life. The first time that somebody comes at me aggressively, I walk away. In my book, hassle just isn't worth it. As you probably know, we have a back lane. The back gardens have gates opening onto it but Mrs Horner's house has a high and blank garden wall and a gate that I've never seen unbolted. So I've taken to walking by the lane except when it's very muddy or I'm in a hurry. There's only a narrow margin of grass and weeds between the track and a field which is usually in pasture, sometimes in grain or potatoes. This year it's oilseed rape. It's not as interesting for a dog as the bushes below the road but at least nobody bothers us and there's no need to pick up dog-plonks. And on the few occasions when I've walked along the road I've stayed on the pavement and kept the old girl at heel until I was past Mrs Horner's house. If I was only dog-walking, I went the other way. There's a path down onto the Moss.

'About a week ago, I had a pint in here before lunch. Somebody kept me talking and I was in a hurry to get home because Betty was going out and she wanted us to have an early lunch. So I went along the pavement with June at heel. I'd hardly set eyes on the harpy for months because of using the lane, but as luck would have it she had opened her drive gate to take out her car and she was just inside her gate. Her gatepost must be a favourite place for dogs to pee and the scent was just too attractive for June, so for once she broke away from heel and squatted to squeeze out a few drops to leave her own signature. You know how dogs do?'

We assured him that we had a very good idea how dogs do.

'She flew at us,' Alistair said. 'She was screeching, 'Shoo! Shoo! Shoo!' Well, that isn't any part of June's vocabulary and the poor old thing was startled out of her wits. She jumped almost out of her skin and dropped a small, dry turd right in the middle of the gateway. I couldn't blame her. If somebody rushed at me, screeching, 'Shoo! Shoo! Shoo!' I'd probably do the same.'

I agreed that my reaction would likely have been similar.

'I usually have my pockets full of polythene bags,' Alistair continued. He dug into a pocket and produced three or four bags, at least two of which had once contained sliced loaves. 'But when I tried to find one and remove the offending morsel I realized that I'd left my jacket at home because of the heat and I didn't have one with me. I tried to explain this. I even asked her to provide me with a bag,' Alistair said indignantly, 'but she pretended not to hear. She just ranted at me. I think she was enjoying herself. She even said that I was still encouraging my dog to mess on her strip of grass, which just wasn't true. The last straw was when she taxed me with walking off while she was talking to me, several years ago. I said that I would have been happy to discuss the matter if she hadn't been so damn rude. And that's when she blew her top and said that I was the rudest person in the village.

'I didn't feel like facing another shouting match so I walked away again. I went straight home, fetched a plastic bag and returned. And — would you believe? — she told me not to remove the object because she was calling Environmental Health and she wanted to show it to them. I wasn't having that. I did my duty and removed the turd like a good citizen.'

'And that ended the matter?' I asked.

'Did it hell!' Alistair said with unwonted heat. 'This came in this morning.' He produced a letter from his wallet. 'From Environmental Health . . . *I have received a written complaint from a resident alleging that your dog regularly fouls roads and footpaths when being walked and that the excrement is not lifted. Section Forty-eight of the above Act makes it an offence for anyone in charge of a dog to allow it to deposit its excrement in certain places including footpaths . . . Any persons who allow it to do so is liable on summary conviction to a fine not exceeding Five Hundred Pounds.'*

'That's a bit thick,' Henry said, 'even allowing for a certain eccentricity of syntax. But, after all, there's no harm done.' I rather suspected that Henry was finding the whole incident rather funny, as I was. It was to seem much less funny later.

'There may be no immediate harm done,' Alistair said, 'except to my feelings, but what if she's spreading her lies around? And what if poor June really does drop a plonk on a footpath some day and I don't notice it? Having been warned once, I could find myself in court.' He took out a tin, produced a small cigar and lit it. I noticed that his hand was shaking.

Isobel had arrived almost unnoticed as we gave our attention to the story. Although she is somewhat younger than Henry her appearance suggests a stereotypical housewife, preoccupied with domestic trivia and good works. Only on closer acquaintance is it revealed that she is a qualified vet, an inspired dog-handler in competition and a fairly good shot. She is also a usually moderate drinker who sometimes goes off the rails. She flashed her unsuitable spectacles at Alistair. 'In court? Alistair, what have you done?'

Mrs Hebden had reappeared behind the bar, apparently in answer to a telepathic message from Henry, who included me in another round before I could stop him. She lingered while Isobel was brought up to date with the latest gossip. The offending letter was handed round.

When the tale was told, Isobel said, 'I wouldn't worry, Alistair. That woman's quarrelled with three-quarters of the village. It was just your turn. She thrives on discord.'

'It's very confusing,' Mrs Hebden said. Like any good licensee, she always tries to see the best in everybody while still suspecting the worst. 'When she has paying guests they often come in here in the evening and they say what a nice lady she is. I've never met her myself. I don't think she's a drinker.'

'I'm afraid she is,' Isobel said. 'I was behind her in the checkout queue at the Co-op in Cupar and she had several vodka bottles in her shopping. If it had been several different spirits I'd have known that she was stocking up for her guests, but vodka's what the secret tippler buys because the smell's easily disguised. When she saw me looking she said that she'd seen me coming out of the pub that morning and I ought to be ashamed of myself — that was the morning I came by to book a meal for that evening. I told her that the bar wasn't open at that time and that she of all people should know that.' Isobel smiled at the memory. 'She was not pleased. She'd have to show her visitors a different face, of course. They come back year after year for the golf or sailing or the wildfowling and they pay through the nose because she really is a damn good cook — or so I'm told — she's never invited me to dinner. She probably needs the money — have you seen that awful old car? — and she'd hate to lose it.'

Another man came into the bar, nodded to us and took a stool at the far end. I knew his face although for the moment I couldn't place him. Mrs Hebden went to serve him.

'Coming back to this,' Alistair said plaintively, brandishing his letter, 'should I do anything about it?'

'Definitely no,' Henry said. 'Don't answer it. You'd be in danger of turning a nothing into a something. Swallow your pride and ignore it.'

I rather disagreed and I was about to advise Alistair to put on record at least a letter denying any such offence but Henry, with a sidelong glance at the newcomer, frowned me into silence.

'And talking of swallowing,' Isobel said,

'John, I was to tell you that your meal's on the table.'

I gathered my dogs and my excess burden of draught Guinness, nodded to the stranger and set off for home.

* * *

The garden at Three Oaks, like the paddock which I had bought with the rest of the property, had largely been taken over by the kennels and their runs, four to a group, and by such other essentials as a large rabbit pen; but we had managed to retain a vegetable plot behind the old farmhouse and some lawns with adjacent beds and shrubberies at the front and one side. Near the corner, beneath a silver birch, a trestle table was installed in fine weather and here, on our motley collection of folding chairs, we assembled next day to take a snack lunch and compare notes. There was just enough breeze to keep midges away but the food had to be covered against the droppings of a family of blackbirds which had claimed the tree above.

Our junior helpers had been excused work for an hour or two to allow the heat of the day to pass and Sam, our young son, had been taken to lunch with a friend, so we were an adult company — very adult in the case of

16

Henry, who had walked over to join Isobel. In addition to Beth and myself were our two kennel-maids, Hannah and Daffy.

The day being Saturday, our house guest was also present. Bruce Hastie was a thin, dark man in his early thirties. He was Beth's cousin and a recently fledged partner in a substantial firm of Dundee solicitors. He was in the process of purchasing a house nearby (to which he hoped to bring his present financée in the fullness of time) but the agreed date for possession was still several weeks away and, in a moment of rare expansiveness, we had offered him the use of our spare room until he could move in. We had rejected his offer to share in the running cost of the household, with the result that he spent much of his evenings and weekends hard at work about the kennels out of a sense of obligation — which was, from our point of view, a far better bargain.

The hot topics were soon disposed of. Macbeth, a huge golden retriever whose owners were holidaying in the Canary Islands, had taken badly to being left in kennels and had been trying to demolish and eat his kennel, his bed and Hannah, but a mild tranquillizer in his feed seemed to have solved our problem; and a potential outbreak of fleas introduced by a so-called Jack Russell terrier (*Jack Russell*, strictly speaking, is a standard and not a breed) had been nipped in the bud. Fleas are a perennial risk in kennels and can spread like wildfire. Owners and visitors are not impressed by an array of furiously scratching dogs and the well-being of the hosts can be seriously affected, so the risk is treated seriously. Isobel will treat any flea-ridden local pet free of charge with preparations of her own devising, arguing that the expenditure is modest and the disruption negligible compared with eternally treating the much larger number of animals on our premises and regularly sanitizing the kennels and runs.

That subject put aside for the thousandth time, there was leisure to chat and I was curious. 'Why did you shush me last night when that man walked into the bar?' I asked Henry. The previous evening, I had told Beth the story of Alistair and Mrs Horner as an amusing anecdote. She must have passed the tale on to Bruce, Hannah and Daffy, because nobody seemed to be in any doubt about the context.

'Didn't you know him?' Henry asked.

'I know hardly any men in the village, except the shooting men and one or two who come into the pub,' I said. 'I know some of the wives who I've met dog-walking, but I couldn't tell you their names, only the names of their dogs.

'It's come back to me that I'd met that chap once before. He came into the pub and we got talking about Devolution and possible Independence. I said that we Scots weren't a nation but a whole lot of tribes who never had got along together. I pointed out that accents and dialects change about every ten miles. He went further. He said that you could tell whether a population considered itself united in nationhood because its songs gave the game away. England and Wales, he said, have songs about the countries but, outside of London, very few songs about places. Scotland and Ireland have few songs about the countries but almost every city and most of the small towns are mentioned in songs. Everywhere from 'I Belong to Glasgow' to 'The Ball of Kirriemuir'. The same, as he pointed out, is even more so in America; and apart from 'Rule Britannia' and 'The British Grenadiers' we couldn't think of a single song about Britain as a whole, which goes to show how much of a nation we Brits are. I've been thinking about it ever since and he's right.

'Be that as it may, and I'm not commenting until I've had a chance to consult the Song Book, the man was Roland Bovis,' Henry told me. 'He has some sort of connection with Mrs Horner. I don't know what, but I've seen them talking amicably enough. Maybe they're related.'

Daffy, without seeming unduly curious, always knows everything about everybody. 'They're not related,' she said. 'He's a neighbour and he's in partnership with her nephew. The nephew lives in Dundee but Mr Bovis moved into the village recently, where Mrs Tolliver used to live, next door to Mrs Horner. The two men have an upmarket antique shop in Broughty Ferry. It says *The Snuff Box* over the door but it's usually known as Shute and Bovis.'

'I know the place,' Henry said. 'I looked in the window the other day when I was over at my dentist. They have some good stuff in the window, but overpriced. The shop looked half empty. If Bovis hadn't walked in on us yesterday, I was going on to say that Mrs Horner's making enemies, right, left and centre.'

Hannah was looking puzzled. 'Is she a stocky, red-faced woman who wears tweedy sort of things even in this weather and puts on good jewellery just to go to the corner shop?'

'Add that she has a face like a frog,' said Daffy, 'and that's the one.'

20

'Well, I've seen her around,' Hannah said. 'And not long ago I bumped into her in the door of the shop. Literally bumped, I mean. She helped me to pick up some things I'd dropped and she was as nice as ninepence.'

I happened to be looking at Bruce. He seemed about to speak but changed his mind.

'Obviously you didn't have one of the dogs with you at the time,' Isobel said. (Hannah shook her head.) 'I gather that she's quite rational on any other subject. A backstabber and a general pain in the neck, but comparatively rational. She just happens to have a phobia about dogs. It's her misfortune that almost everybody else around here has at least one much-loved dog and often more. She's quite capable of stopping some innocent dog-walker in the street and ranting at them.'

Once again, Daffy knew the reason. 'Her husband's sight was failing before he died,' she said. 'Somebody told her about *Toxocara canis* and she got it into her head that that's what he died of. Not that she liked her husband very much, from what I've heard, but he was hers and she doesn't part willingly with anything she owns.'

'Is that what it's about?' Isobel said. 'She got on to me about *Toxocara* once and I gave her the facts. I told her that you can't catch it except by swallowing the eggs excreted by a dog, cat or fox and nobody ever died of it anyway. I said that it's rare for the sight of even one eye to be impaired, that several times more children are blinded by fireworks every Guy Fawkes Night than by *Toxocara* in a year and that all the dog-owners around here religiously pick up the dog-doodies and worm their pets regularly.'

Bruce made a sound of amusement. 'How do you pick up a dog-turd religiously?' he enquired. 'Or are you referring to the power of prayer?'

'You know perfectly well what I mean,' Isobel retorted. 'You lawyers make fortunes by nit-picking over the meanings of words and I suppose it becomes a habit. Anyway, I pointed out that almost every known case of *Toxocara* had resulted from a child playing at home with the family pup, so a little domestic hygiene would accomplish more than all the harassment of dog owners in the world. But I had the impression that her ears slammed shut whenever I said anything she didn't want to believe.'

'Was that this morning?' Beth asked. 'I thought that I saw her old banger at the door.'

'No, it was weeks ago. She brought her old moggy to me for a check-up this morning,' said Isobel. 'I told her yet again that there's nothing wrong with her cat except old age. I gave her some dietary supplements which may or may not do some good. Dogs weren't mentioned or I might have tried again. Honestly, how she has the nerve to rant against dogs, indulge in a good, old fashioned slanging match with me in the street and then bring her cat here, of all places, for veterinary treatment I'll never know.'

'It's nearer,' Beth said. 'And probably cheaper. Well, back to the old treadmill, I suppose.' She began to gather the dishes.

'That cat hates nearly all dogs with a deep and deadly hatred,' Isobel said. 'That may be part of the problem. But that cat, geriatric or not, can see off any dog in Fife.'

'Like owner, like cat,' I said.

★ ★ ★

Behind the house and only one long field away there is a long and narrow wood where, with the full permission of the landowner and the grudging but unnecessary agreement of the tenant farmer, I am permitted to shoot rabbit and pigeon and to train dogs. On a hot afternoon, the wood is more shaded than the Moss, so I gathered my three pupils for the afternoon and headed there.

23

'Little and often' is the prime rule in dog training, and as it was cool under the trees, we were making good progress, and by concentrating on one dog at a time, leaving the other pair attached to a shady tree, I was paying at least lip-service to that rule. The wood was partly open and so was well undergrown with bracken and blaeberries. These were young dogs, siblings, sharing their first experience of being put to hunting a pattern among the heady scents of rabbits. After the first minute or two the rabbits were all underground, but I fired the occasional blank cartridge through the adapter in my shotgun and gave the occasional retrieve of a fur-covered dummy. It seemed that three simultaneous pennies had dropped. My pleasure was second only to that of the dogs and I was glad of the excuse to stay in the shade and ram the lesson home.

Young dogs are easily distracted. I was tempted to suspend the lessons when the sound of footsteps approached, brushing through the bracken on either side of the narrow but well-trodden path. On the other hand, they would soon be expected to work while ignoring all distractions, including the presence of strangers, so I decided to stick to both routine and discipline until the stranger had passed. The newcomer, however, not only made his appearance but stopped to watch while making the little throat-clearing noises of someone who hesitates to interrupt but would like to catch your eye. Before looking round, I sat the dogs and dared them to move again.

The new arrival was a man who I had occasionally passed while dog-training on the Moss. He was a cheerful, tubby man who could have been any age between fifty and seventy but was certainly retired — from one of the professions, to judge from his manners and turnout. I had never seen him without a camera so I judged that he made a hobby of photography and took it seriously, but instead of his usual Pentax I noticed that he was nursing a new-looking digital camera.

'It's Captain Cunningham, isn't it?' he asked.

'*Mister* Cunningham,' I said. 'I stopped being a captain some years ago and I don't see any need to pretend otherwise.'

'And I'm Allan Carmichael.' We shook hands. 'I have a new toy,' he said. 'Do you mind if I try to capture some of the spirit of your dogs?'

'Not in the least, if I can get prints of your best shots. I'm always in need of good photographs and it's not easy to work the dogs while using a camera. My wife usually cuts their heads off.'

'I'll try not to do that,' he said modestly and we passed a pleasant half-hour trying to get each of the dogs to perform to best advantage for the camera. He seemed happy to take shot after shot. 'Film doesn't cost anything,' he explained. 'When I've filled it up, I dump it into the computer and start again.'

'I was admiring your toy,' I said. 'I'll come and admire the prints when they're ready. Where do you live?'

'I live near the Pit.' The 'Pit', also sometimes known as the 'Quarry' is in fact a large sand-pit beyond the Moss which had been reopened recently to supply sand to the building industry. Traditionally this had been obtained from the River Tay, but Tay sand could be very salty, resulting in stained and damaged work. Builders who wished to play it safe used pit sand.

'But,' he said, 'you needn't trouble yourself. Here's another advantage of the system.' And he showed me how the viewfinder was also a miniature viewing screen. He flicked through the pictures that he had taken and I was able to pick out a dozen excellent shots of the dogs at work and at rest. I promised him a duck or a pheasant in due course in return for prints of each. He chose the pheasant and we parted on amicable terms.

When at last I made my way down to the gate between the field and our garden, the shadows were beginning to lengthen and a pleasant coolness was creeping over the land.

Beth met me at the corner of the house. She was carrying a puppy in her arms and had another on a leash. Her eyes were bright with excitement. In a checked shirt and cut-off jeans she still looked like a teenager. 'You won't believe what's happened,' she said. 'I'll tell you later. There are clients waiting — a couple. Their son's a member of a rough shoot and they're thinking of getting a trained spaniel for his twenty-first birthday.'

Beth was quite right, of course. The firm's revenue comes from several sources but the sale of trained dogs comes high on the list. Suppressing any impatience, I spent an hour with the man and his wife. They were quite knowledgeable, only slightly shaken by the cost of a trained dog and satisfied when I explained the months of keep and training that had gone into the product. I put Nepita through her paces on the lawn. They held a whispered consultation and concluded the deal. I agreed to keep her until the great day, but all the while I was wondering at Beth's barely suppressed animation. It could have been due to anything from an outbreak of mange to a phone call inviting us to dine at Balmoral Castle.

I found Beth in the kitchen, struggling to prepare the evening meal. This was due to Isobel who, because she hated the claustrophobic office, had brought the paperwork out to the big kitchen table; and the kennel-maids whose preparation of the dogs' dinners had overflowed from the former scullery next door. Henry, who still had a finger in many pies, was away on business and Bruce was fetching supplies from Cupar or they would have joined the throng and Beth, I am sure, would have given up in disgust. Beth likes but seldom gets the kitchen to herself.

'So,' I said. 'What is it that's happened that I'm never going to guess?'

'Two of the boys came back in a high old state of excitement,' Beth said. 'They've knocked off and gone back to see what they can find out.'

'And that's it?' I asked in the faint hope of goosing Beth into jumping forward to the punchline. I should have known better. Beth tells a story in her own sequence or not at all.

'No, of course that's not it,' she said irritably. 'They'll be coming back for their money later.'

Daffy and Hannah, I could see, were hiding

28

smiles. They always enjoyed my abortive attempts to get Beth to the point. Isobel was more helpful. She looked up from her papers. 'The police were at Mrs Horner's house at lunchtime,' she told me.

'Who's she been complaining about this time?' I asked.

Now that the main storyline was out, Beth was ready to speak out rather than risk losing her audience. She threw Isobel a reproachful glance. 'It must be more than that,' she said. 'Dennis lives in Old Ford Road and he'd taken Steven home to lunch. They say that there were several cars and a tape across Mrs Horner's gate boxing in a bit of the pavement. They went back to Dennis's house, two doors further along, and looked out of an upstairs window but they couldn't see more than just heads over the wall. The police seemed to be milling around in her garden.'

'Sounds serious,' I said. 'Do you suppose she's been in an accident?'

Isobel never hesitates to say aloud what's in all our minds. 'We should be so lucky. Somebody's probably been pinching fruit out of her garden and she's called out all the forces of law and order to trap the culprit. She seems to have a very strong sense of what's due to her.'

'Perhaps she's been running an illicit still,'

Daffy said, 'or growing pot in that big greenhouse.' She went out to call Sam and Audrey, the other two junior helpers, who had been happily cleaning the last of the dog-mess off the grass with the aid of a powerful but odorous machine. Under her stern eye they washed their hands thoroughly and were set to helping with all the dishes and the various diets.

When the four trolleys (ex-supermarket, rescued from the River Eden) had squeaked and clattered away, Beth said, 'They wouldn't tape the place off unless they were searching for something, would they?'

'Probably not,' I said.

Beth inflicted serious injury on an inoffensive courgette from our garden. 'Don't be so aggravating,' she said. 'What do you *think*?'

'I don't think anything,' I said. 'Calm down. I've no doubt we'll have all the rumours in an hour, we'll know which of them are rubbish a day later and we'll know all about everything in the fullness of time. Why waste precious brainpower in guesswork when we don't have enough facts?'

'Because it's when you don't have all the facts that you can believe what you want to believe,' Beth explained seriously. 'When you've got all the facts, the explanation turns out to be about as interesting as a suet pudding.' She was wrong this time, of course.

I went to clean and lock up my gun. When I came back to the kitchen, Bruce had returned from Dundee with several bags of a special puppy-meal and some veterinary products for Isobel. Beth had told him what little we knew and was venturing again into speculation.

Bruce sighed. 'I'd better get over there,' he said.

'Yes,' Beth agreed. 'See what you can find out.'

'I'll certainly do that,' Bruce told her. 'But whatever I find out will probably be in confidence. I'm her solicitor.'

I decided that he was deluding himself. Whatever he found out, Beth would have it out of him before he could hiccup.

Bruce's car was hardly outside the gate when the two boys returned. 'There was an ambulance,' Steven said breathlessly, 'and the police tape is still there.'

'And we could see a lot of men crawling around in the grass and flower beds,' said Dennis.

'They chased us away when we tried to look into the ambulance,' said Steven, 'but Dennis's mum saw them putting somebody inside and she said that the person was covered up, head and all.'

'And she said that means that they're *dead*,' Dennis said in a horrified whisper.

★ ★ ★

The four young helpers finished for the week and were paid off. Three scampered together along the path to the village, determined to plumb the new mystery to its very depths, while Sam, who had put up his usual argument for equal pay for almost equal work, set up another moan at being kept at home. We finished the last of the chores, visited all our stock, the temporary boarders and those in quarantine kennels and, once we were sure that all were well and as contented as could be hoped, we adjourned for our customary knocking-off drink and discussion. The two kennel-maids had come to consider the evening's refreshment as part of their due wages, although to do them justice they seldom asked for anything more than a shandy or a spritzer. As evening approached the midges had become active. Rather than plaster ourselves with repellent mixtures which were only partially effective against what the entomology books refer to as the Scourge of Scotland, we adjourned to the sitting room.

Isobel was in a hurry to get home and

prepare for Henry's return but it would not have been in her nature to refuse a sociable drink. She quickly downed a large gin and tonic while joining in a quick thrash over the day's business activities and set off on foot, refusing the offer from Hannah of a lift home.

Bruce returned a few minutes later and accepted a dilute whisky and a share of the settee. We waited. He seemed to be lost in thought.

'Well?' Beth said at last. '*Well*?'

Bruce sighed. 'I was wondering how much I could tell you. As I said before, I was Mrs Horner's solicitor and I'm also her executor. But I don't have anything to say that won't be public knowledge by morning — if it isn't already all round the village. I never knew such a gossip-factory.'

For some reason, I had been assuming that Mrs Horner had killed somebody in a fit of her infamous temper, but now it seemed that she was the victim. His use of the tenses was confirmation enough. 'How did it happen?' Daffy asked.

'That's the big question. At the moment, the police are thinking of it as an accident but investigating on the assumption that there may have been foul play.

'As it happened, the house was open and I was able to tell them where she kept her will, which was one of the things the investigating officer wanted to know, so I was able to prove my status as executor. The police are always relieved to find somebody to take over responsibility for valuables so, after that, he opened up a bit.

'Most probably it was a freak accident. She drowned in her own water butt. He showed me the place. The butt stands at the corner of her big greenhouse which backs onto the rear lane, partly shaded by an enormous old pear tree. There was an empty watering can nearby which she may have been intending to fill and an overturned box that she may have stood on. When they pulled her out, it was noticed that one of her earrings was missing — garnets — not very valuable but expensive enough. Her ears had been pierced very near the edge of the lobes and one of her earrings had been torn out. Assuming a struggle, they started searching the garden, but the sergeant had a bright idea. He felt in the bottom of the water butt and found an earring which was an exact match to the other. He also found a pair of kitchen tongs which she might have been using to fish around on the bottom.

'The most likely scenario so far is that she was preparing to take water for her greenhouse plants but came too close to a branch of the pear tree and snagged her earring which fell into the water butt. It was about half empty. She fetched the tongs, stood on the box and leaned over to reach down into the water butt with the tongs, but the box moved and she slipped and went head down into the butt. It was of comparatively narrow diameter but quite as tall as the usual run. The water level, of course, rose as she went into it. She wouldn't have had room to get her hands back and pull herself up by the rim and the water was too deep for her to push herself clear of it against the bottom.'

Bruce's voice tailed off. My mind was picturing the scene. It was not the pleasantest of pictures. Some sudden deaths may be merciful. Nature produces its own anaesthesia. When oxygen is cut off to the brain, unconsciousness comes soon and painlessly; but, in a drowning, I have always believed that there must be a period of struggling and breath-holding, of fear and desperation.

'You don't sound convinced,' Beth told Bruce.

'It's not my business to be convinced,' Bruce said seriously. 'There will have to be at the very least a fatal accident inquiry in front of the sheriff. Whatever the due process of law decides, that will be the truth so far as I am concerned.'

'Unless, of course, you're representing somebody who's adversely affected,' I said.

He brushed that aside. 'Of course. Well, it could have happened that way. On the other hand, somebody might have been at hand when she lost her earring and took the opportunity to give her a helping shove. It could even be that they snatched off the earring. Well, we'll just have to wait and see what the investigation produces — the pathologist's report in particular.'

'I thought you said that it wasn't your business,' Beth said.

Bruce had a dry sense of humour, but it rarely showed when his profession was concerned. 'As executor, it's my business to ensure that I don't deliver a legacy to an heir until I can be certain — legally certain — that he or she was not implicated in the death.'

We had had rather more than our fair share of sudden deaths in recent years and I had come to know some of the criminal investigation officers. 'Who's the investigating officer?' I asked. 'Burrard?'

Once again, Daffy had all the facts. 'Inspector Burrard retired,' she said. 'He's up in Aberdeen now, doing something in security for BP.' She looked up at the clock. 'I'll have to leave in a minute. Rex will be home in a couple of days and the cottage is a mess, so don't let me take root.'

'It's an Inspector Blosson,' Bruce said. 'I gather that he's had a recent promotion and is trying to make a name for himself. I don't think that you'd like him very much. A self-righteous man. Rather too self-assured for my comfort, though he was almost obsequious today. I think he could be a bully if he had the advantage over somebody.'

'They won't leave a newly promoted inspector in charge of a suspicious death for long,' I said.

Bruce nodded. 'That's what concerns me. He may be in a hurry to assume foul play, make an arrest and close the file before he finds somebody put in over his head.'

'And then,' said Daffy, 'in about twenty years somebody will decide that the conviction was unsafe and there'll be an apology and compensation and a witchhunt for the real culprit. And the original accused will have been guilty all the time. We've seen it all before.' She finished her shandy and made her departure, stepping out like a man but swinging her hips under a very short skirt like a woman.

'She's becoming very cynical,' Bruce said disapprovingly. Any criticism of the machinery of the law he considered to be his own prerogative.

'She always was cynical,' Beth said. She grinned suddenly. 'Believe it or not, her views are becoming more tolerant. You didn't know her five years ago. She was *weird*. Now she's a respectable married lady, more or less. Who found Mrs Horner's body?'

'A youth,' Bruce said. 'He doesn't seem to be involved. He was passing by and he heard the cat sounding distressed. He ventured inside the gate, very cautiously in case the lady leaped out at him, but after only a step or two the water butt came in sight — I can vouch for the geography — and he saw a foot.'

'But who was the boy?' Beth asked.

'Francis something.'

'Francis Earl?' I suggested.

'That's the one.'

An ancillary mystery was explained. Francis had been one of our first junior helpers. He was older now and becoming preoccupied with girls and exam results, but girls are expensive and we had been expecting him to come and help with the elementary dog-training. It had been unlike him to let us down without explanation.

'Another thing,' Bruce said. 'Would you like Mrs Horner's estate for a client? I have her cat in my car. I could hardly leave her to starve. She's a placid old thing. Can you board her until I can find her another home? I don't think she'll be any trouble as long as she can eat and sleep and has somewhere to defecate.'

We had one house cat. Over the years we had suffered pressure from good clients to board their cats as well as their dogs, so that we had been forced to create a small cattery in a shed beside the barn. It was, I thought, empty now.

I glanced at Hannah. She shrugged and got up. 'She won't have been fed. Is your can locked?'

Bruce looked appreciatively at her departing back. 'That's more my idea of what a kennel-maid should be,' he said. He paused and pursed his lips. 'I don't know whether I should tell you about this but you may be able to tell me what it means, if anything. Mrs Horner had left two letters on her hall table, ready to take to the post. The Inspector, with my agreement, opened them, hoping, I suppose, that she might have mentioned that 'So-and-so just arrived and is going to look at my water butt with me.' But no such luck. He decided that they were of no interest and handed them over to me as executor.

'Each was addressed to one of the local papers and each was complaining about the misbehaviour of dogs. But what the Inspector failed to notice was that they weren't on her own notepaper and didn't even bear her own address. One was ostensibly from a Miss Langley of Newburgh and the other from a Henry McNab in Cupar. But each seemed to have been typed on the old Corona on her desk.

'As her executor, it's my duty to carry out the wishes of the deceased, but she never actually said that she wanted them posted. If she's taking somebody else's name in vain . . .'

'I doubt that very much,' I said. 'I think those are fictitious people. There have been a lot of letters in the local rags recently stirring up anti-dog feelings about noise, smell, droppings in the street, danger of attack, you name it. And each complaint seemed to bring a fresh spate of letters in support. They may all have come from the same pen — or typewriter.'

'The old *bitch*!' Beth said.

2

The Sunday which followed showed every sign of passing peacefully. There was still police activity at Mrs Horner's house, though at a reduced level — or so we were told. Sunday was always a day of less activity at the kennels, a day for hurrying through the essential tasks, perhaps tackling any projects deferred due to lack of time but in general giving the dogs and ourselves a respite. Our junior helpers, who worked as much for the fun of it and the love of young dogs as for the money, would cheerfully have come in, but on the day of rest they were firmly excluded in the interests of family life and to avoid alienating the devout.

Daffy had taken the day off in order to prepare her cottage and her delectable person for the return of her husband Rex from his job offshore. Hannah, who would carry an extra load while the usually workaholic Daffy was on short hours for Rex's benefit, had a date with her latest boyfriend and dashed off as soon as the morning chores were finished. Bruce went off to collect his fiancée and take her to watch him compete in a clay pigeon meeting near Perth and on the way he dropped Sam off in the village. Sam had an invitation to spend the day at his friend Audrey's house. Audrey was nearly ten as against Sam's seven years, but the two were becoming devoted friends. Beth was inclined to worry in case they got themselves talked about.

Isobel had gone to Edinburgh with Henry to visit an old friend from Henry's merchant banking days, so for once Beth and I had the place to ourselves. We gave the dogs the minimum of essential human contact and then spent a delightfully lazy afternoon, dozing at first in deckchairs and then pottering in the garden. Bruce had intended to be back in good time to help with the dogs' meals, so there was no urgency. The earlier we started the work, the more we would have to do unaided. We looked at each other and no words were needed.

With the room next door occupied by Bruce and the partition walls being not very thick, we had felt inhibited. Since my illness sex had not been very high on my list of priorities, but I was beginning to feel that nostalgic pang that says desire is on the way.

We came in out of the brightness and heat into cool dimness and climbed the stairs.

'Bruce will come back before we're done,' Beth said.

'Then he can get on with the dogs' dinners,' I told her. She grinned at me wickedly.

We undressed, cleaned ourselves up and settled down. We were very slow and gentle and loving. Recent abstinence made the newly recovered joy all the sweeter. We were both nearing climax when we heard a car on the gravel.

'That'll be Bruce,' Beth whispered. 'Don't stop now.'

Another car arrived. There were angry voices, none of them sounding in the least like Bruce. I found that desire had escaped me.

Beth knew it as soon as I did. 'Come back as soon as you can,' she whispered and gave me one of her special kisses.

I dressed quickly and went downstairs on slightly shaky knees. Alistair Branch was in the hall, glaring defiantly at two strangers. He saw me on the stairs and he was speaking before I had descended two more steps.

'John, is Bruce Hastie here?'

'I'm expecting him back at any moment.'

'Damn. Can I wait?'

'Yes, of course,' I said — reluctantly, because I had somebody special waiting for me upstairs. The larger of the other two men I suddenly recognized as the sergeant from the village — a new posting whom I did not know well. He was in civilian garb, jacketless but very neat in a white shirt and a tie. The last thing I wanted was to become embroiled in Alistair's problems at that or any other moment, but he was Henry's friend and he was in trouble. 'Can I help?' I asked.

The smaller man broke in before Alistair could speak. He may have seemed small next to the sergeant but as I came down the last few steps I saw that he was as tall as me and undoubtedly heavier. At first glance, despite a prominent nose and bushy eyebrows, he looked inoffensive but looking again I saw that there was a twist to his mouth and a slant to his cheekbones which somehow, in the intuitive way that one guesses character from casts of features, made me think that I would neither buy a car from him nor sell him a puppy. 'Really,' he said in the voice of one more hurt than angry, 'there's no need for this. Mr Branch may be an important witness and we have one or two questions . . . I'm Detective Inspector Blosson and this is Sergeant Morrison.'

Alistair was shaking, but whether from fear or temper I could only guess — I thought possibly both. 'They have a dozen questions and most of them seem to be suggesting that I'm guilty of something and they won't say what and I'm not answering any more until I have my solicitor with me.'

'Mr Branch,' said the Detective Inspector, 'we made no such suggestions.' His accent, I decided, was definitely Glasgow, faint but not from one of the better areas.

Alistair continued to address me. He was visibly distraught, his colour high and his face looking pinched. 'They keep asking me to explain things I know nothing about,' he said. 'They say there was another dog-turd in Mrs Horner's gateway. I've told them and told them that I picked up the one June dropped that caused the row with Mrs Horner and I haven't walked along the pavement in front of her house since. And there's something about a cigar. But I'm not going to be badgered. And they were trying to get me to go along to the District HQ at Cupar but I'm damned if I'm going to walk into their parlour unless Hastie says that I should.'

Sergeant Morrison was holding his book against the wall and was writing laboriously. 'Would you speak more slowly, please,' he said.

Alistair threw the sergeant a hunted look. 'I'm going home now,' he said. 'Betty's very upset. When Hastie gets back, tell him what

I've said and that I'm not saying another damn thing until I've heard from him.' He pushed past the Detective Inspector and left the house. The two policemen left without another word and I heard both cars drive off.

I turned and went up the stairs, two at a time.

★ ★ ★

Bruce returned about twenty minutes later, which just gave Beth and myself time to recover the mood and bring matters to an unhurried and satisfactory conclusion. I dressed quickly once again and descended to meet him. He was bearing a very small medal and seemed highly pleased with himself. I probably appeared equally complacent, because he looked at me curiously.

His mood took a tumble when I led him into the sitting room and described the recent visit, quoting the dialogue as accurately as I could. 'There's no doubt that they were talking about Mrs Horner's death?' he asked me.

'None at all. They'd been asking him about dog shit in the gateway.'

Instead of rushing out and galloping to the rescue, Bruce collapsed into a chair. 'Well, here's a pretty pass,' he said.

'What's wrong?'

'Alistair Branch has been a client of the firm for years. In fact, it was he who suggested that I buy Broomview. And I'm Mrs Horner's executor. As executor, can I act for someone who may be suspected of having a hand in her death?' The question was rhetorical so I held my tongue. 'It hasn't come to that yet,' he continued. 'I'd better go and see what it's all about. I'll see you when I see you.'

'That seems probable,' I said.

He went out to his car. I dragged myself back upstairs. Beth was lying on her back, one arm across her eyes but the rest of her deliciousness exposed. I kissed her on the navel. 'Don't say that you're ready again?' she said sleepily. 'I'm flattered.'

'The spirit would be willing,' I said. 'The flesh, unfortunately, is not. Listen, Bruce has rushed off to give aid and comfort to Alistair.'

'So we still have the place to ourselves?'

'We also have the dogs' meal to ourselves.'

Beth sat up suddenly and looked at the clock. 'Yikes!' she exclaimed. 'And we'll need something to eat as well.'

'I could phone Daffy,' I suggested.

'Daffy's busy. Let her be the last resort. Phone one of the juniors. I suggest — Francis.'

'I thought you might,' I said. It was Francis who had found the body.

* * *

Francis lived two doors beyond the pub and on the same side of the road. He answered the phone and said that he would be happy to come and help out. He sounded only too pleased to be rescued from Sabbath boredom. Sunday, he often said, was the sort of day that gave God a bad name.

He arrived by bicycle so promptly that Beth had barely finished getting dressed. He was a tall, thin boy with fair hair and a nervous disposition but he had blue eyes, good teeth and no spots, so that I could well imagine girls showing interest in him. The ladies of the firm were inclined to mother him.

We had no very young pups at the time, the youngest dogs being old enough to get by on two meals a day. Even so, catering for the multitude, on diets varying in quantity and content, was a complex and laborious procedure. As the business had grown we had learned to streamline our techniques, but nothing could reduce the volume which had to be measured out and transported. Our plans for a food store and servery central for the kennels had disappeared into the offices of the Planning Authority and vanished, apparently for ever.

When the last dish was emptied and the last water bowl filled, I went to feed and reassure Mrs Horner's cat. She was a handsome beast, a ginger — unusual for a female. She woke up for long enough to empty the dish, squatted and scratched for a few seconds. I parted the fur behind her ear until I spotted a small group of fleas. She seemed to appreciate a little human companionship but soon tired and went back to sleep again.

Francis was in the scullery, washing the stainless steel dishes and conversing with Beth through the open door. 'Francis's parents are in Perth today,' Beth told me. 'He was going to have to make his own meal. His mother left him some cooking instructions which he can't even understand. Really,' Beth said irritably but with a wink to me, 'it's time that boys were given lessons in domestic economy or whatever they call it these days. I've told him that he can stay and eat with us — Bruce phoned and he's having dinner with Alistair and Betty, so we have enough to go round.'

I said that that was fine. I thought Beth would have found some other excuse to retain

Francis for a little ladylike brain-picking on the subject of Mrs Horner had his parents not been so obligingly elsewhere.

I fetched a sherry for Beth and a Guinness for myself. Francis accepted a shandy — my usual offering for the under-age drinker. We took our seats at the kitchen table while we waited for the potatoes. The meal was otherwise cold.

'You'll be getting your name in the papers,' Beth said. I had to admire the obliquity of the approach. An immediate demand for information can raise the hackles or tie the tongue.

'The reporters have been after me already,' Francis said, not without a modicum of quiet pride. 'I told them as little as possible.'

'Oh?' I said. 'Why?'

'I like Mr Branch.'

My eye met Beth's. 'I don't quite follow,' she said. 'How does it affect Mr Branch?'

'Tell us the whole story,' I suggested. 'We've only heard bits of it and we may be getting it a bit garbled.'

Francis brightened. I thought he might be glad to have found some sympathetic ears. 'All right,' he said. 'I'd been for a walk out by Old Ford Road and I was heading for home again.' Francis paused and looked bashful, wondering whether we knew that the current object of his devotion lived in Old Ford

Road. He hurried on. 'I usually used to scoot past Mrs Horner's house, because you only had to sneeze and she'd be out having a go at you for spreading germs, just about, but this time I heard her cat yowling so I stopped and took a couple of steps in through the gate, ready to run if she appeared.

'There's a bushy sort of evergreen opposite her gate, beside the garage. It hides the greenhouse and most of the garden, but as soon as I stepped inside I could see a pair of feet. They were sticking out, about a metre off the ground, not moving, and it looked kind of . . . '

'Unnatural?' I suggested.

Francis thought about it and shook his head. 'More than that. Impossible. I mean, it's not the sort of thing that ever happens. So I took another couple of steps and had a better look and I could see that it looked like Mrs Horner's bottom half and her top half was down in the water butt. The cat was walking round in circles and making a strange noise. There was a wooden box nearby and it looked as though she'd been reaching down into the water butt and slipped or got stuck. She didn't seem to be moving at all but I thought that she might have given up the struggle for the moment, so I went closer.'

Francis broke off. He was very white but I

could see a thin film of sweat on his face which the warmth of the day did not explain. 'I was sure that she was dead,' he said in a hushed voice. 'The water was almost up to the rim of the butt. I wanted to lift her, in case she wasn't quite dead, but I was sure that she was and I had never touched a dead body, never even seen one. So I dashed home — it's only a few yards — and told my dad. He phoned for an ambulance and then went to look for himself, but on the way he met the local policeman, Sergeant Something — '

'Morrison,' Beth said.

'That's right, Sergeant Morrison. He came with us and he more or less took over. And he came to take a statement later and he said that I'd done just the right thing. My dad said the same. But I can't help wondering if she mightn't have been saved if I'd pulled her out,' Francis finished miserably, his voice breaking. He put his head in his hands.

'Almost certainly not,' I said, not caring about the facts but just trying to relieve his mind and give him a little time for recovery. 'And if she'd already been dead for some time, the police would have been cursing you for disturbing the scene. They like the evidence left alone if the person's dead or an immediate attempt at resuscitation if there's any life left. How the untrained passer-by is supposed to know the difference, nobody has ever explained.'

Francis dug out a rather grubby handkerchief and gave his face a wipe before straightening up. 'I'm sorry,' he whispered. 'May I use your bathroom?'

'Carry on. You know where it is,' I said.

He was back in a couple of minutes, washed and looking better. I thought that the telling of the tale again in less formal surroundings might have helped him. His parents had probably adopted the don't-talk-about-it policy which is often very much the wrong one. 'I'm sorry,' he said again. 'You must think I'm soppy.'

'Not a bit of it,' Beth said stoutly. She got up and began to pour the water off the potatoes. 'The idea of death is frightening enough, especially when you're young and have everything to look forward to. You think that it will never come to you, so seeing it and having to face up to the fact that we're mortal and will all end up that way some day is an awful shock. And there's an atavistic instinct to be afraid that something dead will suddenly move. You know what atavistic means?'

Francis nodded. I was relieved. I would not have liked to have to define it myself.

'You say you had to make a statement?'

Beth asked. Francis nodded again. 'What did you say in it?'

'Pretty much what I've just told you.'

'Oh, come on!' Beth said. She managed to sound as though she was totally incurious and just kidding him along for his own sake. 'There must have been more than that. What questions did they ask you?' She seemed to speak absently while she prepared to serve the meal but I knew that she was absorbing every word.

'Funny sort of questions, some of them, but they made me remember things. Like . . . I didn't really take it in at the time but it came back to me later. While I was up close to her, I noticed something on her back. Well, sort of just above her bottom, where she was highest. There was some ash. I don't mean like burned paper, I mean a neat little stick of ash like tobacco ash. It would have been rather big for a cigarette, probably a small cigar. It looked as if somebody had leaned over her while he was smoking and the ash had dropped onto her. When the sergeant took my statement he picked me up rather sharply about that, as if he wanted me to say I'd made it up, but I hadn't. I think,' Francis said sagely, 'the trouble was that he'd moved the . . . the body and never noticed the ash and what I said made him look an idiot who'd disturbed the evidence without even seeing it. Later, when I heard what people were saying, I realized that I might have got Mr Branch into trouble because he's the one who usually smokes those little cigars around here and I tried to withdraw my statement, but that inspector wouldn't let me. He wanted me to say that I'd seen Mr Branch walking along the pavement with June earlier in the day, but I wouldn't because I didn't. And he asked me if I'd seen a dog plonk in Mrs Horner's gateway, but by then I'd realized that Mr Branch was in trouble, or at least he could be made to look as if he was, because it's all over the village that he had a row with Mrs Horner over a dog plonk in her gateway, and I could see what they were getting at, so I said that I hadn't. But I had, really. It's gone now,' he added.

'Yes, it would be,' Beth said. 'Don't think about it any more. Would you like some chutney?'

Francis shook his head. 'I don't think I'm very hungry after all,' he said.

★ ★ ★

At Three Oaks, we are heavily outnumbered by dogs and so we live our lives by the timetable most suited to their nature, which means that we are usually very early to bed and early to rise. Bruce, like most lawyers, tended towards the other extreme. As a result, we did not see him on the Sunday night. We left a note and the makings of a milky drink for him on the kitchen table and went to bed.

Next morning, some time after our day's work had begun, he came down for his breakfast looking grim but determined. Beth had made it clear from the start that she had no intention of knocking off work to cook him breakfast at a time when her thoughts would soon be turning towards the preparation of lunch, but Beth and I were not above joining him for coffee in the kitchen while he consumed his cereal followed by the toast and marmalade which was the summit of his culinary ambition.

When we told him that Detective Inspector Blosson seemed determined to incriminate Alistair by connecting the dog doo found on Mrs Horner's premises with June, he took the news calmly. 'Mr Branch found that out for himself the hard way,' he said. 'That eternally damned Detective Inspector said that he's sending the dog plonk and a small cigar butt that they found in the garden for DNA testing and he asked Mr Branch what he thought of that. There's no answer to that sort of question, of course. And then he asked whether Mr Branch had any objection to samples being taken from himself and his spaniel bitch for comparison. He could hardly say anything but yes.'

'Then what's the problem?' Beth asked.

'The problem is that DNA results can be indeterminate. Or they can be tampered with. And, anyway, it came out recently that it's just possible for two people to show identical DNA profiles. Dammit, I must find out whether it's permissible for me to act for him. With a modicum of luck, one of the other partners will have to take over. Meanwhile, it might be helpful if we knew what questions the police have been asking and, more importantly, what answers they've been given.' He raised his eyebrows.

'Well, don't look at us,' I said. 'We're not PIs.'

His eyebrows rose even further, giving his face a still more comical look. 'I'm not looking at you as possible investigators,' he said. 'If you went around in this extraordinary gossip-factory of a village asking serious questions, the police would hear about it before the day was over. But you have several youngsters working for you as casual labour — quite contrary to the Children and Young

Persons Act — and boys and girls are *expected* to go around asking irritating questions and nagging until they get the answers, and especially on matters that they're not supposed to know anything about. Tell them to find out who told the police what. They'll throw themselves into it, you'll see. With a bit of luck we may be able to head the investigation away from foul play and in the direction of accident.'

'Isn't it a bit premature for that sort of knee-jerk reaction?' I asked. 'Alistair isn't accused of anything yet.'

'It's never too early,' Bruce retorted. 'Memories fade — or become confused — particularly if somebody sets out to confuse them. The earlier we get the picture firmed in people's minds, the better.'

'You may be firming a picture that you won't like very much,' I pointed out.

Bruce paused and thought about that while he finished his coffee. 'I may not like the picture if it's of a policeman trying to put ideas into the minds of witnesses,' he said. 'But I very much want to know about it.'

He drove off towards Dundee in sombre mood, leaving us to speak to our young helpers, who had been enjoying biscuits and milk or Coke in the barn. Sam had been joined by all the other four of our regular helpers — Dennis, Steven, Audrey and Francis.

It seemed to be up to me to set the ball rolling, little though I wanted to become any more deeply involved. I gathered the juniors together on the lawn and brought Daffy and Hannah into the discussion, just in case. I explained to the youngsters that something had happened to Mrs Horner. This did not seem to cause any surprise and I guessed that at least some of the children's families had been commendably frank on the subject and that death had become a mere facet of life and lost its power to horrify. Mr Branch, I said, was being harassed on the assumption that he had done something to Mrs Horner. We only wanted the truth, I explained — the real truth and not what somebody wanted to be the truth. I stretched our remit from Bruce by adding that we would like to know where everybody was during Saturday morning, whether anybody had behaved in the least unusually or out of character and which of the locals had had a recent and serious quarrel with Mrs Horner. 'And for Pete's sake,' I added, 'don't stir up any hornets' nests with questions. Be discreet. Be casual. Or just listen.'

It was a happy chance that each of them lived within a stone's throw of Mrs Horner's house (not that, in our small village, anyone could live much further away). Alistair Branch was popular, handing out sweets or coins with a liberal hand and so, quite apart from the children's natural desire to indulge their curiosities and make bloody nuisances of themselves, they were immediately enthusiastic about the prospect of helping his cause.

Sam, the youngest, was to be allowed only a limited role. (I had in the past been inveigled into helping with the investigation of crimes and, because criminals prefer their misdeeds to go undetected, my life had more than once been endangered as a consequence. I had no intention of the same thing befalling Sam.) The others would have rushed off to begin enquiries forthwith, loss of earnings notwithstanding, but I insisted on the bulk of the day's work being finished first.

Hannah volunteered to make one further enquiry at the shop.

We could have treated ourselves to a quiet day until feeding time came around again. Daffy and Hannah could cope with the routine. Beth attacked the garden. Isobel was at the kitchen table, updating her paperwork and struggling with the field trials entry form for You. (The nickname You was short for Eucalyptus but, despite causing endless muddles with a now retired stud-dog named Yew and worse confusion in the field — a cry of 'Come here, You' might be answered by a whole pack of dogs — it had stuck.) You's registration papers had not yet come back from the Kennel Club, but he was one of our next hopes for Field Trial Champion.

I had planned to take him into the wood for some extra polishing but just as I was gathering up my training aids I was forestalled by the first of a series of interruptions. A young couple had come in search of a pup old enough to begin training. The man was half sold on one of our young dogs but his wife fell in love with it for all the wrong reasons and they left with the pup, a lead, collar, whistle, basket and all the toys and training aids I had ever managed to stock.

Feeling slightly richer, I was hoping to set off again. But another visitor had arrived in the meantime and was waiting patiently in the background. Not a purchasing client this time, I thought. I recognized the man who had come into the pub on the Friday evening — Roland Bovis as I now knew him to be. He was of average height but inclined to plumpness except for slightly sunken eyes. Beneath a mop of curly, black hair, his face was jolly and even in repose had the expression of a small boy wanting to be friends. He was rather better dressed than would be usual in a country village, but I supposed that for an antique dealer an air of affluent respectability would be an essential. He had an elderly Airedale with him on a lead.

I led the way to the chairs under the birch. In hot weather we keep a bucket of fresh water there for the refreshment of visiting dogs and before taking a seat the man waited for the Airedale to drink before it collapsed onto its side, panting with the heat.

'This is Blitzen. Poor old chap,' Bovis said fondly. 'He's twelve, you know. We've had some good years together. I don't suppose he'll have many more, but he comes with me everywhere while he still can. I thought he'd enjoy the walk from the village but he does feel this heat. So do I.' He fanned himself with a copy of the *Fife Herald* that Beth had left on the table. 'Is your cat safely out of the way?'

'He was sleeping on the stairs, last time I saw him.'

'That should be all right, then.' Bovis half smiled. 'Blitzen's a peaceful old boy. Only cats can rouse him into any semblance of his former energy. He hates them all with an uncompromising hatred. All but one, that is.

He gets on all right with my neighbour's cat, which is even older than he is. A pair of geriatrics together, I suppose. But when he isn't in the car with me he spends his days in a secure garden, sleeping away the hours, well away from cats. It's sad when they get old.'

There was a short silence. He patted his brow with a large, white handkerchief. 'You're not at the shop today then,' I said to stir him into life.

'I'm mostly the buyer,' he said. 'I work a lot of evenings and weekends, attending auctions and visiting junk shops, so I leave the shop to the others. That, indirectly, is one reason why I came. The other is . . . that!' He indicated Blitzen, who was making an effort, impeded by the stiffness of age, to scratch his own chest. 'He seems to have picked up a flea somewhere.'

'You want Isobel,' I said. 'I'll fetch her in a minute. What was the first reason?'

'I need a businessman with a shotgun certificate, and you were the nearest one I could think of.'

'Go on,' I said warily. This kind of approach sometimes leads towards matters which are close to the far edge of the strictly legal and I was beginning to feel that his air of openness and honesty was a little too cultivated to be true. The army is a great educator when it comes to spotting frauds and line-shooters and I was not going to put my shotgun certificate at risk for anybody.

'On Saturday, there was a sale in Kirkcaldy — the contents of a big house near Anstruther. There was some good stuff there. To cut a long story short, there was a hammer-gun in the sale. Well, these days guns and shooting are becoming dirty words in the towns. There was a reserve price of two hundred on it and nobody else was bidding, so that's what I paid for it. But when I went to collect my purchase they wouldn't let me have it without a shotgun certificate. They said that it was the law.'

'It is,' I told him.

'Well, it's a damned nuisance. I wondered if you'd pick it up for me and we'll split any profit we can make on it.'

At that moment Audrey passed by, leading two pups. I asked her to invite Isobel to join us. 'If the gun's clapped out and out of proof,' I told Bovis, 'you probably paid too much. You'd have to have it deactivated by a Proof House, which doesn't come cheap, and then sell it as a wall hanger. What name's on it?'

Bovis looked pained although I would have thought that an antique dealer must become hardened to the occasional piece of bad news. 'I don't think it's clapped out,' he said. 'It has those barrels with a pattern. What do you call them?'

'Damascus?'

'That's right. They look to be in good order. I'm not an expert but I couldn't see any dents or scratches. And I know a piece of good figured walnut when I see it. The name Macnaughten was on the rib.'

I pricked up my ears. The Macnaughten action was the direct forbear of my Dickson. 'I can get that organized for you,' I said. 'Henry Kitts goes through to the Borders regularly and he knows one of the top dealers in antique guns. Shall I fix it all up?'

'Please do.' He paused and I saw the first traces of guile peeping out of his honest eyes. 'You needn't tell him that you're in for a share of the profit. I won't tell him if you don't. Just let me know the figure before accepting it, that's all I ask.'

I could well imagine him charming an old lady and getting a bargain of a piece of eighteenth-century silver discovered among her electroplate. 'You'd better phone the auctioneers,' I said, 'and tell them to hold it until one of us calls by.'

'Mr Kitts has a shotgun certificate?' Bovis asked.

'Probably the first one ever issued,' I told him.

65

Isobel chose that moment to arrive in answer to my message. 'Henry would sue you for that,' she told me severely. 'Good morning,' she added. 'I think you're Roland Bovis.'

'Correct,' he said. They shook hands. 'I'm told that you're the flea expert around these parts.'

'That's not my only talent,' Isobel said, 'but it'll do to be going on with. You're sure that it's not mites, or a tick? This old chap, is it?' She bent down and parted the hair along Blitzen's back. 'Hullo, has he come across a myxied rabbit recently?'

'Oh Lord!' said Bovis. 'Don't say that he's picked up something even worse than a flea! He had a good look at a dead one on Friday, near Perth. I let him out of the car for a leg-stretch and of course he made a beeline for the foulest object he could find to roll on. Why do you ask?'

'Nothing terrible. He has a few rabbit fleas,' Isobel said.

Bovis leaned down and looked where Isobel was looking. 'You must have marvellous eyesight,' he said. 'How do you know they're rabbit fleas? I can only see tiny specks.'

'But they're black specks. Dog and cat fleas are brown. If the rabbit had been dead for

66

some time, its fleas would be desperate to transfer to something living. Don't worry, they don't usually stay long, but I'll give you something to make sure of it.'

'While you're messing with your witch's brews,' I said, 'Mrs Horner's cat is also having a scratch. Her specks looked black to me.'

'She may have got them from Blitzen,' Bovis said. 'They're good buddies and Blitzen was also the only dog that Mrs Horner would let inside her gate.'

Isobel gave a sigh, taking the importation of parasites as a personal affront. She produced a small bottle from her overall pocket and deposited a few drops between the hairs on Blitzen's nape. 'I'll give you some insecticidal shampoo,' she said, 'just to make sure. That was a shock, your neighbour dying like that.'

'It was sudden,' Bovis said. 'And possibly accidental but quite possibly not.' He gave an ostentatious shudder. 'It doesn't bear thinking about.'

'You were on quite good terms with her, I understand.'

Bovis stiffened. 'I used to help her out when she needed a man about the place, if that's what you mean. I quite liked the old thing. At least her malice was usually honest and she never went for anyone who couldn't answer back. I had no reason to kill her. All the same, I'm not sorry that I was away all day on Saturday.'

'I didn't mean that at all,' Isobel said, distressed. 'I never suggested such a thing.'

Bovis, at least partially mollified, led his aged canine companion haltingly away but the interruptions were not yet over. I had already collected the dog, my gun and a bag of training accessories when I was hailed by name from the direction of the road.

The newest arrival was a sallow man wearing, despite the heat, a plastic mackintosh and a tweed hat. If he knew my name and also my dislike of being called 'Captain', the probabilities were that he knew me and, although it may be true that More know Tom Fool than Tom Fool knows, I had a vague sense of having encountered him in the past. Such feelings of déjà vu only too often turn out to be from having seen the other on television or even on a 'Wanted' poster, so it seemed prudent to wait, with eyebrows raised, for his approach.

When the stranger identified himself, I recalled him immediately. His name was Jeremy Faulds and he was a reporter with one of the Scottish papers. On a previous occasion when violent crime had touched our community, he had given the story thorough coverage; but where he could easily have sensationalized our peripheral role to our embarrassment and possible disadvantage he had instead been fair and factual.

Isobel, recognizing the smell of the Press, had vanished indoors, leaving me to face any inquisition alone. I saw no need to do so while standing in the sun holding about a stone of assorted equipment. I led the man and the dog back to the seats under the silver birch and deposited my load on the table.

'It's been a few years,' he said as he folded down into one of the chairs. 'And now you've lost a good neighbour.'

During these last few seconds, I had totted up the pros and cons of wising up the Press and had decided that limited revelation might be to Alistair's advantage. I met Faulds's eye. 'Not attributable?' I said.

He shook his head and made a note in a small book which he produced apparently out of thin air. I knew that my name would not be mentioned.

'If you've done your homework,' I said, 'you'll know by now that the lady concerned was universally disliked. She revelled in unpopularity.'

He considered me for a moment. He might be honest, as reporters go, but he was wondering how to get the maximum of information out of me. In the end, he decided on the direct approach. 'Who, in particular?'

'When I said 'universally',' I told him, 'I meant it.'

He grinned. His teeth were very uneven. If I had seen them at first glance I would have remembered him immediately. 'I could reply that when I said 'Who, in particular?' I meant that. I've been getting a similar sort of reaction wherever I've been. Nobody wants to mention names.'

'I'm one of them,' I said. 'Ask around but don't ask me.'

There was a pause. 'Who is Alistair Branch?' he asked suddenly.

'A very placid, retired gentleman who had the misfortune to live in the same road as Mrs Horner. You've heard that he had a run-in with her. But so what? You only heard about it at all because we were discussing it in the hotel a few days ago and the story went the rounds. But as far as I'm aware, the police are still investigating and will probably conclude that she died accidentally.'

'That's not the hint that I've been getting.'

'I can't help that,' I said. My mind had been working on its own parallel track and I thought that I could see a way to steal an advantage. 'And if they do decide that somebody gave her a helping hand into the water butt,' I said, 'at least a dozen others had just as strong a reason to dislike her. I did, to name but one.'

He grinned again. 'Can I quote you on that?'

'I think I'm about to give you something and demand a little coverage, but I'd still like my name left out of it. Wait here a moment.' I gave You the signal to stay and hurried into the house. Bruce, I remembered, had left the two letters from Mrs Horner to the newspapers on the sitting-room mantelpiece and must have forgotten them because they were still there. I carried them into the garden.

'You knew that she had a bee in her bonnet about dogs?' I asked Faulds.

'Yes. But that doesn't make her unique.'

'In a way,' I said, 'it does. The papers, yours among others, have been carrying letters by the dozen, all complaining about noise and teeth and danger to health and everything else that dogs ever get blamed for.'

'Well, then — '

'These were found in her house, ready for the post. Both typed on her typewriter.' I gave him the letters. 'These are typical,' I said. 'You'll see that they purport to come from other people but I'm prepared to bet that not

71

even the addresses are real. You'll also see that one of them — to your paper — pretends to be in support of an earlier letter which she almost certainly wrote herself. You could check that.'

He read both letters several times and pursed his lips. 'And this gives you a motive?'

'Dogs are my livelihood. And my life. Anything that hurts them hurts me. Unfortunately, from your point of view, I didn't know any of this until after she was dead.'

'It certainly throws a little light on her character,' he said slowly.

'And on the letters,' I said. 'I expect you to compare these with the originals of the others and to tell your readers that you've been fooled by false complaints.'

'My editor may not go along with that,' he said.

'Tell him that, if he doesn't, I'll suggest to the Press Council that he's been having his own staff write dummy letters to whip up public feeling against Man's Best Friend.'

'You wouldn't!'

'I bloody well would,' I told him. 'But think for a moment. You now have a newsworthy opportunity to pontificate about the dead woman's deviousness and spite. It'll send a ripple through the other papers, but you'll have had it first.'

Bruce's partners, he told us, saw no objection to his acting for Alistair as well as being Mrs Horner's executor. He would be spending several working days in the village, inventorying Mrs Horner's possessions and going through her papers as well as keeping a protective eye on Alistair.

In a way, this suited us rather well. I had no wish to become involved in receiving the real or imaginary evidence produced by our young helpers, especially at Three Oaks and during working hours when I might be expected to pay, albeit modestly, for the time entailed. I appointed Francis to gather and tabulate the information and told him to report direct to Bruce at Old Ford Road. Francis approached this duty with great seriousness, borrowing for the purpose his father's laptop computer.

With Bruce spending most of each day with Alistair or within a few doors of his house, we might have first heard of the next development only through the grapevine. On that Tuesday, however, Bruce had returned to join us for our evening meal. Isobel, Henry and Daffy had gone to their homes so, counting Sam, we were only five at table. Bruce was too discreet to refer to a client's affairs unnecessarily. Beth, I could tell, was desperate to ask whether there had been any developments, but she feared a snub if her cousin retreated behind his professional ethics. Thus our mealtime conversation wandered randomly over a vast range of topics, from politics to religion to superstition, to penal reform and so back to politics again. Sam was allowed to join in provided that his remarks were to the point and, in fact, his views were the most strongly held of any although I thought that I could detect some of my own more entrenched arguments among his. He was at the age when a boy is most certain that his own opinions are indisputable. Some never grow beyond it.

We were interrupted as we were finishing our meal with locally grown strawberries and ice cream. We heard the patter of frantic feet running, almost staggering, from the direction of the road and up to the front door. Hannah was first to her feet but before she could get to the front door it had been pushed open and a small figure stumbled through the hall and into the kitchen. With some difficulty, I recognized a lady whom I had sometimes seen around the village.

We all jumped up quickly. Somebody pushed a chair behind her and she was lowered into it. She seemed unhurt but she was shaking as if palsied and she was panting like an overheated dog.

'Mrs Branch,' Bruce said, 'what's wrong?'

It happened that I had never met Alistair's wife but she seemed well known to the others. She dabbed at her hair, which was in wild disarray. 'Wanted you,' she gasped to Bruce. She snatched several deep breaths. 'Can't drive.' Two more breaths. 'Ran all the way.'

Beth rounded on Sam, who was listening, goggle-eyed. 'Go and get ready for bed,' she told him. 'Now!'

'But Mum!'

'Go! But Betty,' Beth said, 'you could have phoned.'

Betty Branch nodded violently and drew several more breaths. She was holding both hands to her chest. Having partially caught up with her oxygen debt she was ready to speak. 'I knew Mr Hastie was staying here,' she said, 'but I didn't have the number and stupidly I couldn't remember your surname. It's Cunningham, of course. I remember now.'

She struck an immediate chord with me. Since my illness, my memory for names always deserts me in times of crisis. 'We are in the yellow pages,' I pointed out.

'I never thought of that.' She dabbed again

at her hair and pulled at her disarranged blouse before turning back to Bruce. 'Mr Hastie, they've arrested Alistair. That mannie Blosson came back with two other men and they gave Alistair some sort of warning and they took him away and I didn't know what to do so I came straight to you.' Her voice broke.

Beth caught my eye and mouthed 'Brandy'. I had just had the same thought. It is our sovereign specific for all sicknesses and disasters. I hurried through to the sitting room, poured a generous measure and returned.

'There won't be much that we can do at this time of night,' Bruce was saying, 'except to remind him not to make a statement until I'm with him. If they've arrested him, and if he was given a formal caution — it sounds as though they would certainly have done that — they won't be letting him walk out just yet. Let me run you home and we'll make up a bag with what he'll need — pyjamas and so on, nothing expensive — and I'll take it to him and see what's going on. Did they say where they're taking him?'

'Cupar, I think they said.'

'That would be likely. Will you be able to manage? Do you have anyone who could stay with you?'

Mrs Branch had been sipping the brandy and seemed to be sitting straighter but now she slumped again. 'My son's in Canada,' she said helplessly. 'I have a sister in Hereford, but she couldn't come right away.'

'Would you like me to come and be with you tonight?' Hannah asked her.

'Oh, would you, my dear?' The older woman's lip quivered. 'I couldn't face it alone. Alistair wouldn't do anything like what they're saying. He just wouldn't. You all know that, don't you?'

Dutifully, we all said that we did.

'But what *are* they saying?' Bruce asked. 'Did they give anything away?'

'That man,' said Mrs Branch — and there was a whole world of contempt in the words — 'he said that they had the D-something results and the post-mortem report and Alistair had some serious explaining to do.'

Bruce was frowning. 'I thought that DNA tests took ten days or more,' he said. 'In fact, I was counting on it.'

I knew something about DNA tests due to the occasional paternity dispute — in connection with dogs, I mean. 'That's the usual waiting time,' I told him. 'The tests themselves don't take long if they jump them to the front of the queue.'

'So they treated them as urgent. I wonder

why. No doubt time will tell. I'll try to arrange bail tomorrow. They sometimes allow it, even on . . . this sort of charge,' Bruce said carefully. The word *murder* was not to be bandied about in the presence of an already distraught wife. 'But it may be difficult. Come along, ladies. We must get organized.'

'I hate that policeman,' Alistair's wife said. '*Hate* him! He thinks he can just trample over everybody. And — do you know? — I'm sure I've met him before. His face . . . And even more his voice . . . '

After a short delay while Hannah collected her overnight necessities, Bruce carried the two women off. Beth and I were alone. We gathered the dishes. As we stood at the sink, Beth said, 'I suppose we do know that Alistair wouldn't do such a thing?'

'Henry might know it,' I said. 'We can ask him tomorrow.'

3

I awoke next morning with a dully aching tooth. The first contact with the cold milk on my cereal triggered an explosion of full-blown toothache. A phone call to my dentist's number only produced the information that he was on holiday for ten more days. I took two paracetamol and got on with my life. As often as not ills cure themselves, although this is not so commonly true of teeth.

Daffy, whose husband was still at home from his oil rig, was into one of her periods of irregular working hours. Hannah, who would usually have made up for Daffy's absence by starting with a furious burst of energy at the crack of dawn, walked in late for work in the morning, explaining that Betty Branch had been reluctant to lose her company and had found excuse after excuse to detain her. She had only escaped, Hannah explained, by promising to return that night and to send Bruce along to lend his support as soon as he was up and about.

Henry had arrived with Isobel. Even in what must surely be his twilight years, Henry's mind was still sharp and clear; but he was past the time of life for intensive physical work, so we were glad of our helpers. Beth and I had fed the younger dogs. We left the juniors to get on with the cleaning and walking and foregathered over Bruce's breakfast table for coffee which I dared not risk taking.

'Human teeth are nature's greatest failure,' I grumbled. 'We should have had teeth like the guinea pig's which keep on growing and have to be cut back now and again.'

'Some people wouldn't bother to cut them until they were sticking out in all directions,' Henry said. 'Would you like me to phone my dentist?'

'For God's sake do,' I said. Now, to add to my other woes, my mind was filled with pictures of my friends and acquaintances, all with teeth 'sticking out in all directions'.

Henry phoned his dentist, who had a slot available later in the morning.

Beth put her question to Henry as soon as he was back at the table. Was Alistair the sort of person who might boil over and kill somebody?

'Of course not,' Henry said stoutly. 'I've known Alistair for years. He's a gentle soul, the very last I could imagine committing an act of violence. When he was in insurance, he could reject a claim or foreclose a mortgage with the best of them, but it was always done with as much consideration as circumstances permitted so that the loser ended up feeling almost as though Alistair had done them a favour. That, I think, is why he was successful — clients came back to him time and again. Not always the ones that he wanted, but business is business. Now in retirement, he has to psych himself up to complain about a poor meal in a restaurant.'

'That's all very well,' Isobel said. 'But anybody can be pushed beyond endurance. The most unlikely people do sometimes go off pop and do something out of character. And then,' she added, 'the neighbours all say they knew all along that he'd do something like that.'

'Under the sort of provocation that Mrs Horner seemed to enjoy handing out,' said Beth, 'Mother Theresa would probably have blown her top.'

The discussion might have wandered into anecdotes about Mrs Horner's ill-doings, but Bruce dragged it back. 'You're missing the point,' he said. 'Alistair Branch is my client and so he is definitely and absolutely as innocent as a newborn babe until proved guilty.'

I looked at him, but he was perfectly

serious. 'After which,' I suggested, 'he's as guilty as hell?'

'Not necessarily,' Bruce said. I began to recover my respect for the legal mind but he forfeited it again. 'Not if we decide to appeal.'

'How does the evidence look?' Henry asked him.

Bruce turned down the corners of his mouth. 'It doesn't look too good but it's early days and they're releasing details with all the enthusiasm of a hen laying a brick. I'm told the DNA results show that the turd came from June and the cigar stub showed traces of Mr Branch's saliva. That went on the record, so it's probably true.'

'That's rather damning, isn't it?' Hannah said.

'Not necessarily. I'm hoping to find out more today. I'll take Mrs Branch along for a visit and do some serious stirring up to see what I can find out. What do I look for in the DNA evidence, if I can get at it?'

I deferred to Isobel's superior knowledge of biochemistry. 'They must have been very small samples,' she said. 'A trace of saliva and a few cells from the wall of the anus. It's not much to work with. Were there enough points of similarity? Like fingerprints, they need a minimum number of points of similarity to constitute proof. Offhand, I forget how many.

If the sample's small enough, they could probably find similar bits of pattern shared between almost any two examples. And, of course, the sample could be contaminated by the DNA of whatever meat went into the dog food.'

Bruce put down his cup and frowned. 'Could it really? After passing through a dog's digestive system?'

Isobel shrugged. 'I haven't the faintest idea, but you might be able to use it to shake their over-confidence.'

'Got you. Does your child labour have anything for me?'

'Some of them do, I believe,' I said. 'But I doubt if you'll get it if you refer to them as child labour. It's locked up in the laptop computer that Francis is carrying around most of the time. He can print it out for you in the office, if you like.'

'I'll have to rush,' said Bruce, who had been taking his breakfast as though there was nothing in the world but time. I had noticed that although he was at ease with his contemporaries, he had a shyness with young people, who recognized his vulnerability immediately and, with the innate cruelty of their kind, played it up. 'Ask Francis for me, will you, please?'

As Bruce's car started up, I said, 'I just

don't have time to get involved in any more investigations. And, frankly, I don't give a damn who killed Mrs Horner as long as it wasn't one of you. It wasn't, was it?'

Isobel shook her head impatiently. Beth did not dignify my question with an answer. Henry said that he hadn't thought of it.

'I'll have to get moving if I'm going to keep that appointment,' I said. 'Henry, Alistair's *your* friend. Speak to Francis, would you? Tell him what Bruce wants.'

Henry brightened. There's nothing he welcomes so avidly as an excuse to pry into a mystery.

A sudden pang like a hot electric worm in my tooth reminded me of my troubles. I changed into a more respectable pair of trousers and set off in the car. Rush hour was past so that there were none of the usual tailbacks around the Tay Road Bridge. I drove east, parallel to the north bank of the wide estuary, and turned down off the Arbroath road into Broughty Ferry.

I was soon able to guess why Henry's dentist had been able to take me at short notice. She turned out to be a capable and not unattractive young woman. The more old-fashioned Scots hesitate before trusting a young woman, however attractive, in any of the traditionally masculine professions. I felt happy in her hands. The young make up for any lack of experience by having mastered the latest techniques; and women dentists, in my experience, are more sympathetic to the male sufferer. She had my tooth excavated and filled in short time without inflicting on me any more discomfort than the prick of a needle and, with a few words about coming back if it gave me any further trouble and to try to chew on the other side that day, she sent me out into a brighter and altogether better day.

On my way to the dentist from where I had parked the car, I had been too distracted to pay much attention to my surroundings. Now, looking around with freshly unclouded eyes, I saw that I had walked past two antique shops. One, the smaller and less prosperous looking, bore the name *The Snuff Box* above the window.

I paused for a look. In my fresh mood of bonhomie, I thought that I might pick up a present for Beth. As Henry had said, the window held a few good pieces. On a very handsome table were set out a Delft dish from the mid seventeenth century, a Liberty art nouveau pewter teaset and several globe-and-shaft wine bottles. But these would undoubtedly be priced higher than even my present mood would allow.

My watch told me that I could spare a few minutes so I went inside. There was nobody in the shop but I guessed that the large mirror on the far wall was probably a transparently silvered one-way mirror. Not that there was much to guard inside the shop. The stock on show was mostly little better than rubbish. The one good piece was a chest, apparently of walnut. Out of curiosity, I opened a drawer. As I thought, oak.

'You're quite right,' said a voice behind me. 'It's been veneered, probably during the twenties.' I turned to find a woman closing the back-shop door behind her. 'Why, it's Mr Cunningham!' she said.

'Judith Tolliver!' I replied. The numbness in half my face distorted my voice but I thought that she would probably recognize her own name. 'I didn't know that you were in the antiques . . . ' I nearly said *racket*, then *trade*, but finished . . . 'business.' Judith was in her late thirties, tall, slim and dark. Her looks were good, only flawed by bushy eyebrows which she adamantly refused to pluck. She and her husband had lived in the village until he was killed one winter night when an oncoming car had skidded on a surface of polished snow and slammed into him. Ironically, the other driver had escaped with minor scratches. Beth and I had exchanged invitations with the Tollivers on occasion and I remembered that their house had been furnished very tastefully with what Judith told us was a mixture of genuine antiques and reproductions. She was a born chatterbox but otherwise charming.

'When Jim died,' she said simply, 'I was left with very little money, a nice house and some good antiques. That's how I came to meet Roley Bovis. I was just making coffee. Would you like a cup?'

'Yes, I'd love a cup. I've just been to the dentist,' I said, 'but if I scream and rush outside you'll know that the anaesthetic has worn off suddenly.'

She took me into an office where we sat on either side of a battered desk on chairs which creaked mournfully. As I had thought, we had a view of the shop through the mirror. She poured coffee from a modern percolator. 'If your mouth's still numb,' she said, 'be careful not to burn yourself.'

'I can manage,' I said. 'I have feeling on one side. Of course, I remember now. Mr Bovis bought your house.'

'He saved my bacon, financially speaking. He got me this job and they let me sell my better bits and pieces through the firm on commission. I have a small flat near the Lifeboat Station with a view across to

Tentsmuir and I get by.'

The coffee was delicious, more so because I had not managed to take much breakfast. 'Do you enjoy the job?' I asked her.

She shrugged. 'I know something of antiques and I'm learning all the time. I think I have a knack for selling.'

Something in her voice made me say, 'But?'

'But I don't know how long it'll last. Ian Shute's the businessman and we do the selling between us. Sometimes people walk in off the street with something to sell, but Roley Bovis does the rest of the buying and sometimes he gets caught out.'

'Fakes?' I suggested.

'Sometimes. And he spent the earth on a Minton royal service from Balmoral which turned out to have been stolen. I shouldn't be telling you all this.'

It was my turn to shrug. 'I could have guessed most of it from the contents of the shop,' I said. I could visualize the unhappy picture. Credit already overextended, the few good pieces marked too high because cash was needed. 'You may be able to buy your old house back cheaply.'

'I wouldn't mind that,' she said, 'now that the old witch is dead. I felt guilty — would you believe? — selling the house to Roley without telling him of the awful neighbour, but as it turned out they got along like two lovebirds. Even at the time of the bust-up . . . '

'When Mrs Bovis walked out?' I asked.

'There was a bigger one than that. Mrs Horner brought in a pair of fake Georgian candlesticks, her one heirloom. We got her quite a reasonable sum for them, but she'd convinced herself that they were genuine and that there should have been another nought on the end. In fact, Roley had taken them to an auction for her; but nothing would suit her better than to blame Ian and me. Then, when Helena Bovis decided to change partners for the dance of life and moved in with Ian, Mrs Horner took Roley's side against her own nephew. From what I heard, she was much more indignant than he was. In fact, he was more relieved than anything.'

I had to wait, nursing my still hot mug of coffee, while she went into the shop and sold a brass door knocker to a pair of holidaymakers. When she settled again she said, 'The papers hinted that the police suspect foul play.'

While I had the ear of one who knew the inner circle so intimately, I could hardly turn my back. 'It's gone a bit further than that,' I said. 'They've arrested Alistair Branch.'

'Oh no!' She seemed genuinely horrified.

'That nice old man! Did he do it?'

'None of us believe so.'

'And no more do I. But I suppose . . . '

'What do you suppose?' I asked.

'I suppose,' she said, frowning, 'that Ian would have been a more logical suspect if he hadn't been out of the country. They're sailing in the Adriatic, did you know?'

'So I hear,' I said.

'Well, it's true. He phoned from Venice on Saturday morning to ask whether I thought we should stock Venetian glass. I said that we have good crystal in Scotland, lower priced than Venetian. After all, we aren't having to pay for keeping Scotland from sinking slowly beneath the waves.'

Before I left, she sold me a nice little Victorian brooch for Beth and sent her her love.

★ ★ ★

I spent what was left of the working day shuttling to and fro between the kennels and the wood with a series of dogs, either our competition hopefuls or those who would be offered for sale as fully trained for the approaching season. I deafened myself firing dummies from the launcher and I blew my whistle until my lips chafed,

90

but whenever I came back to the house I could hear the voices of Francis and Henry in deep discussion.

By late afternoon I was weary but pleased with the afternoon's progress. I lent a hand with the animals' evening meal and gave Mrs Horner's cat some food and a few minutes of companionship. She had stopped scratching, so either Isobel had worked her usual magic or the old cat had decided that the effort of scratching was more bother than the occasional itch. When I headed for the house I saw Bruce's car outside the front door. I sneaked in quietly. I was hot and leg-weary after so much exercise in close weather, my cotton shirt was sticking to me and the anaesthetic was wearing off. I wanted little more out of life than a shower and a change of clothes, to be followed by a cold drink taken sitting down.

I came downstairs twenty minutes later, already partially refreshed, and headed for the sitting room. Bruce and Henry were in possession, hunched over a drift of small papers on the coffee-table, but I was not going to be kept out of my own sitting room and away from my own drink by visitors. I helped myself to a can of beer, sat down and poured.

'Is it that time already?' Henry asked brightly.

I sighed. I might be refreshed but I was still physically weary. 'Help yourselves,' I told them. 'I wasn't going to disturb you.'

'We noticed,' said Henry. 'Go ahead and disturb us. We'll forgive you.'

I settled back in my chair. 'Did the responsible young citizens who you lightly refer to as child labour produce anything useful?' I asked.

Bruce got up to do the honours. As he poured he said, 'Observation seems to have been remarkable for its absence, but having had a good look around I can guess why.'

I thought that I could see what he meant. 'The local shop only keeps tobacco and magazines and a few essentials like bread, milk and eggs,' I said. 'So, on Saturday mornings, most families go to do the week's shopping in Cupar or Dundee. Or the husbands may go golfing or sailing. In this heat, there was probably an exodus to the beach at Tentsmuir. The place was as quiet as a morgue.'

'So the place was half empty,' Bruce said. 'It was also half full. But those who were still here were mostly hugging the shade. And even that isn't the whole explanation. I never noticed before, but when the leaves are on the trees you can hardly see the houses in Old Ford Road and those houses look over the Moss at the front and farmland at the back. Old Ford Road only has houses on the right as you enter it and the road curves to the right. The plots are big and there are trees along most of the boundaries, so they're mostly hidden from each other at the front. Across the road there are more trees and the bank down to the burn. At the rear it's more open after the wall round Mrs Horner's garden — beyond that it's all clipped hedges and a fence to the track along the edge of the field.

'To cap it all, when the trees are in leaf the one place in the village street from which you can see at least part of the way along Old Ford Road is at the bridge where the burn passes under the street, just where the pavement's very narrow. Nobody ever lingers there.'

While Bruce was speaking, Beth and Hannah had appeared in the doorway, ready to foregather for the end-of-working-day drink and debriefing. They hesitated quietly rather than interrupt and perhaps make him lose the thread of what he was saying, but when he looked round and came to a halt they found seats. Bruce, the perfect guest, again rose to act as barman. Isobel joined us before he had finished and there was a squeezing-up on the settee. Daffy had visited and helped out with her usual explosive energy but had vanished again.

'Were you saying that our — um — junior staff couldn't help?' Beth asked as Bruce settled for an upright chair.

'No, I'm not saying quite that,' Bruce said. 'Just that circumstances were against them and there are large gaps in the information just where we wouldn't want them. Frankly, a herd of camels could have wandered around Old Ford Road that day with only about a ten per cent chance of anybody noticing.' He paused and looked around thoughtfully. 'I don't see why I shouldn't pick your combined brains,' he said at last. 'I wouldn't be revealing anything that won't be the subject of endless gossip within a day or two. Conversely, your local knowledge may suggest how to fill some of the gaps and you'll also know what those gaps are if you get the chance to pick anything up in conversation.'

I was on the point of objecting to becoming an unpaid inquiry agent but Henry, Beth and Hannah were obviously pleased. Isobel, however, shared at least some of my reservations. 'Aren't you rushing things a bit?' she suggested. 'Surely, it will be ages before Alistair can come to any trial and by that time

94

the facts will all be out in the open.'

'The facts are never all out in the open,' Bruce said. 'Only the ones brought up in evidence. Whether they'll be the right facts is open to argument, which is what advocates are for. What's more, Mr Branch will have to be brought before a sheriff for a committal proceeding shortly. There'll be a small delay because, what with holidays and a slipped disc, they're having difficulty providing enough sheriff court time. But the point is that, although I'll ask for bail, it would be unusual and the police, at least as far as the Inspector is concerned, intend to oppose it. Once he's committed for trial he'll have several months in a remand centre to look forward to. How would you enjoy being taken out of circulation and into a cell, to await a trial for something you know you didn't do?'

'Not a lot,' I said. There was a murmur of agreement.

'When you're young,' said Henry, 'a month is for ever because it's a large percentage of your life so far. When you get old, it becomes a growing percentage of the time you've got left.'

'I'll take your word for it,' Bruce said. 'The best chance of saving Mr Branch from that fate would be to convince the police or the fiscal's office that they don't have a case, before the committal proceedings.'

'A thin chance, wouldn't you say?' asked Hannah.

Bruce shrugged. 'I've done it before. Once. Maybe I can do it again. So let's make a start.' He began to shuffle through his papers.

'If you say so,' Hannah said. 'I'll kick off, shall I? It's not much help. Mr Cunningham asked me to call at the shop so I went in to buy a roll of Polos. The news of Mr Branch being arrested was all over the place. I only had to mention his liking for those small cigars and it all came out with very little prompting because Mrs Branch had bought sixty — six tins of ten — to take to him. That cleaned them out, but it didn't matter because he was the only regular purchaser and they'll have some more before he gets through sixty.'

'A pity,' said Bruce. Henry gave a grunt of annoyance.

'But,' said Hannah, 'and it's a big but, the reason they were short of them was because Mr Jordan also bought several tins last week to hand around. He said he wasn't going to waste good cigars to celebrate a fifth grandchild, born in Tasmania to an estranged daughter-in-law who couldn't even be bothered to send him a Christmas card.'

'So anybody, any man for miles around,

could have had an unsmoked one available,' Bruce said. 'That's just dandy!'

'But surely,' Beth said, 'if Alistair's DNA was on the butt — '

'I'm not so worried about that,' Bruce said. 'We can argue that anybody could have picked up a butt. It's the ash that worries me. Let's move on.'

'I did my bit. I paid a visit to the pub,' said Henry.

'Of course,' Isobel put in.

Henry ignored the interruption. 'The news doesn't get a whole lot better. On Saturday morning, Alistair looked in early and had a quick pint. He had June with him. He bought a bottle of cheap white plonk — '

'Plonk can't be anything but white,' I put in. 'It comes from *vin blanc*.'

'Don't nit-pick. Where was I? Alistair said that Betty was trying out a new recipe and he only had red wine in the house. He soon left, saying that Betty was in a hurry for the wine. Mrs Hebden had made a statement to that effect and also repeated Alistair's story of his quarrel with Mrs Horner. She told me that she didn't mean to say anything about it but it just slipped out.'

Bruce sighed and then shook his head. 'What it is to be garrulous! The fact that Mr Branch was in a hurry and therefore had a

97

reason to go by the front way doesn't mean that that's the way he went, nor that if he did walk by the quicker way he encountered Mrs Horner. He is adamant that he returned by the track on the other side of the houses. He also adds something very significant. He says that as he passed Mrs Horner's garden wall he heard her voice saying, very loudly, 'What on earth are you doing?' I was in two minds whether to advise him to include mention of that in his statement. In the event it turned out to be immaterial, because Mr and Mrs Pelmann, in the next garden along Old Ford Road, heard it too.'

'The Pelmanns don't live in the house next door,' said Hannah. 'They live about three houses further on. The house next to Mrs Horner's belongs to some people called . . . called . . . '

'McIntosh,' said Beth. 'I only know that because they called and asked if we would keep their daughter's pet rabbit while they're away. I said that we weren't equipped for domestic rabbits.'

'All of which may be perfectly true,' Bruce said, 'but doesn't alter the fact that the Pelmanns were in the garden of the house next door, belonging, as you so rightly insist, to the McIntoshes. Apparently, they were asked by the McIntoshes, who have a summer cottage in the Dordogne, to look after the house and garden in their absence. Unfortunately their eyes were down because, taking their responsibilities seriously, they were weeding a rockery and their hearing was focused on the television in the sitting room beyond the open French windows. According to their son they were waiting for the qualifying session for the Formula One race to be broadcast, intending to get home before the actual qualifying period began. But at least they were keeping an eye on the time and they agree that when they heard Mrs Horner's voice it was eleven twenty-five, give or take a minute or so. They saw nobody go by and heard nothing else. The inspector thinks that that fixes the time of death but the pathologist gives a rather wider margin.'

'This is all very well,' Isobel said, 'but aren't you missing an important point?'

'Very possibly,' Bruce said. 'But which one?'

'The point is that if Alistair didn't have an uncharacteristic fit of temper and if the death wasn't an accident, whoever did it must have been a local who knew Alistair's habits and had heard the story of his quarrel with Mrs Horner. Almost certainly someone who had watched his comings and goings. She was a quarrelsome woman, much given to making enemies. Were the Pelmanns numbered among them? They, of all people, could have seen Alistair go by and have witnessed the dropping of a cigar butt and a doggie doo.'

'As far as we know,' Bruce said, 'the Pelmanns rubbed along well enough with Mrs Horner. She made enemies, true enough. You yourself, John — '

'I had words with her,' I admitted. 'She referred to Ash as a bandy-legged, flat-faced, flea-infested, evil-tempered pug. But I don't know that you could call her an enemy. An ill-wisher, perhaps.'

'There are plenty of those. And there is at least one person who benefits from her death.'

'That will be the nephew,' Henry said.

'You didn't hear that from me,' Bruce said stiffly. 'Mr Branch remembers seeing the Pelmanns but reached his own back door, next after *Chez* MacIntosh, without seeing or being seen by anyone else. Mrs Dalton, mother of Steven, was in her kitchen with the window open and she heard Mrs Branch say, 'Hello dear,' but she's rather vague about the time or even the day. Her husband was away in Wormit, pottering about in his yacht.

'Francis, the boy who found the body, visited the last house in the road — ' Bruce scrabbled through the notes. 'Incidentally, he never did explain to my satisfaction what he was doing in Old Ford Road that morning.'

For once, mine was the local knowledge because I had several times shot in Brian Jordan's company or picked up behind him. 'The last house is that of a Mr and Mrs Jordan,' I said, 'and their daughter Clare. Francis fancies himself very much in love with Clare, who doesn't know that he exists and doesn't want to know.'

'That doesn't explain what he was doing in Old Ford Road.'

'Of course it does,' Henry said. 'Gazing at the outside of the loved one's dwelling.' Henry had been young once, a very long time ago.

'It's such a shame,' said Beth. 'Audrey, one of our junior team, would do anything for him but Francis ignores her.'

'Which is probably just as well,' Bruce said, 'if she'd do anything for him. But whatever Clare may think of him, her mother obviously favours his suit. She opened up to him. At eleven twenty-seven a lorry went past, coming from the sand-pit. She knows the time because she heard the telephone ring while she was in the bathroom and by the time she reached the phone it had stopped, but her answering machine gave her the time of the message. She could hardly make out the words for the noise of the vehicle. The driver may have seen somebody. I'll follow it up.'

'Some of the houses along the village street look across the field. Somebody may have seen something,' said Hannah.

Bruce shuffled his papers and produced another page. 'Our team of investigators hasn't made progress along there yet. The house on the corner, backing towards Mrs Horner's gable, has a walled garden matching hers so there wasn't a lot to be seen. The house is from about the same period as the houses in Old Ford Road. They think that the next two houses along the village street were empty at the crucial time and only the first one has any sort of view towards the Old Ford Road houses. Beyond that there's a rise in the field which cuts it off. They had gumption enough to look across the field from the back of Mrs Horner's house and that was their conclusion.'

'The house on the corner belongs to Roland Bovis,' Isobel said. 'He lives there alone — his wife left him earlier this year.'

'I think you can pass him by,' I said. 'He was at an auction in Kirkcaldy on Saturday. Which reminds me, Henry. He bought a Macnaughten hammer-gun because it was going cheap and he wants somebody who has a certificate to uplift it and deliver it to that dealer down in the Borders where you do your trustee bit. It may be rubbish or it may be the bargain of a lifetime, we won't know until we see it.'

'I know the dealer you mean,' Henry said, 'and I'll be heading that way fairly soon. But Kirkcaldy's rather out of my way. Can't we get it picked up before then?'

'We'll see what we can do,' I said. 'I'm promised a share of the profit, so if it comes off I'll cut you in.'

'No need for that,' Henry said. 'I've had my share from you already in free booze. Apropos which . . . ' He held up his empty glass.

★ ★ ★

I sat and tried to do some constructive thinking about the business while the others picked away at the edges of the mystery without making any further progress. It was impossible to remain detached while around me the discussion was raging and I found myself drawn back into the argument. Eventually, a sense of exhaustion took over. My mind and, I think, those of the others rebelled against weighing up neighbours, visualizing them picking up a late-middle-aged female by the hips and stuffing her head first into a water butt. By tacit agreement we drifted off the subject. It was not until the next morning that anything new emerged.

There had been a long-awaited storm in the night — lightning and at times almost simultaneous thunderclaps followed by a short period of heavy rain. The sunshine had returned in the morning, but benevolent and without the humid closeness of the previous few days. Suddenly the weather was just what weather should be, not too anything. Birds were bathing in the lingering puddles. Small, puffy clouds sailed across the bluest blue. Colours were brighter, breathing was easier and most of the world was in holiday mood. Not the farmers, who had suffered laid cereal crops and the seeds knocked down from the oilseed rape. I too was grudging in my pleasure — the beautiful day had infected the dogs, who wanted to play rather than work and had to be allowed to blow off steam before they would come to order.

Anger would have put at risk much of the progress already made. I used up most of my reserve of patience taking each dog undergoing training onto the stubble of winter wheat beyond the garden gate for a quick reminder of what had gone before, reinforcing my leadership of the pack. I was replacing the last dog in his kennel, with a sigh of thankfulness that the worst was over and that by tomorrow they would be in a more receptive mood, when Beth called me to the phone.

'Mr Williamson,' she said. It was enough. Andrew Williamson was the tenant farmer of the land behind Three Oaks, a crabby, elderly man who resented the ready permission which I had received from his landlord to shoot and train dogs on the farmland. He also had a profound contempt for every breed of dog other than working collies and believed them all to be potential sheep-worriers only awaiting an opportunity to get off the leash.

I took the phone. 'Hello.'

'Captain Cunningham?' He always called me *Captain* although, or perhaps because, I had made it clear that I would rather be addressed as *Mister*. 'Ane of your dugs is rampaging among the sheep again.'

'It's never happened yet,' I said, 'and it's not happening now.' Such incidents had never been down to dogs in my care and I could be certain that every one of them, apart from two being walked by our helpers and which I could see through the kitchen window, was safely kennelled.

'Aye it is,' he said. 'I was awa to shoot the bugger. Then I minded you saying you'd sooner dae it yersel. So come on and I'll be watching to see it's done richt.'

That was not how I remembered our previous discussion but he had hung up before I could say so. I was tempted to call him back and tell him to do his own dirty work. But if I turned my back it was probable that some perfectly innocent pet would be shot. If there really was a savage dog among his sheep and he tried to carry out the execution himself with his .22 rifle, which was almost as old as himself, the most likely outcome would be a seriously injured dog to be put down. If it had to be done, I would indeed prefer to do it myself.

I fetched my .243 Anschutz deer rifle and a few cartridges from the gun-safe and set off up the long slope towards the farm buildings, following a track beside an overgrown hedge. There was a stile at the top which let me onto the tarmac farm road.

Williamson was waiting for me at the corner of his barn, a gleam of triumph in his narrow eyes and his rifle under his arm. Despite his age he was wiry and fit. He led the way along the farm road to a tubular gate beyond which was a large pasture. 'There!' he said.

There must have been two hundred sheep in the field and not one of them was paying any attention to a spaniel which was patrolling the further hedge. 'That is not one of my dogs,' I said, 'and it's not worrying your sheep.'

'It was worrying them, I'm telling you. Now go ahead. Shoot the bugger.'

'I'm not going to kill a perfectly innocent spaniel just because you don't like other people's dogs. And if you harm it, I'll be pleased to give evidence on behalf of the owner. What's more, I could make a damn good guess whose dog that is.'

I took out my silent dog-whistle. I was fairly sure that Alistair Branch had stuck with the signals to which June had been trained. At the first set of pips on the whistle I saw the distant dog's head come up. I waved and whistled again and in a flash she was eating up the ground as a spaniel can.

Williamson fondled his rifle. 'If you take aim at that dog — ' I began.

He sneered. 'You'll what? Shoot me?'

'No.' I stooped to be nose to nose with him and stared him in his watery eyes until he looked away. 'But I'll take it off you and bend it over the gatepost. And don't think the fact that you're decrepit will stop me.'

He seethed. For comfort, I reminded myself that one would have to be very unlucky to be killed by a single .22 bullet, but he kept his rifle properly pointed at the ground. I could hear him muttering threats but I tuned him out.

The spaniel came on and slithered to a halt in front of me on the gateway mud, panting and slavering. I saw the light die out of her eyes as she recognized me. She sat, quivering, and held up a paw. It was an urgent plea for help if ever I saw one. I bent down to give her a pat. Her heart was beating furiously.

'This is Alistair Branch's dog,' I said.

'*Damn!*' he exploded. 'I should hae shot the bugger mysel wi'oot calling you.'

'You know that he's been arrested in connection with Mrs Horner's death? His dog's only been out looking for her master.'

Mention of Alistair seemed to feed his venom. 'When I heard it, I thocht I'd be rid o the bastard for good. Aye walking up beyond the march there an the dug coming onto my land. It can seek for ever, far's I care. Yon Mrs Horner was a fine wumman, aye polite an freenlie when she came to buy a lamb for the freezer. An aye paid cash,' he added as though that incitement to tax evasion alone entitled her to a halo.

For some reason, I had envisaged Mrs Horner living a hand-to-mouth existence, lacking the ready cash to fill her freezer. 'Really?' I said.

'Aye. Just the other week, she was here. She'd had me kill and hang the lamb for her but she came an took it awa an did the rest hersel. A fine wumman. Showed proper respect for an auld man, nae like you, ye bugger. She'd nae mair use for fancy dugs than I hae.' He snorted in the direction of poor June. 'She'd been tae the polis, she telled me, an laid a complaint against a dug that bit her while she was oot walkin an a summons was served. Determined to hae the dug destroyed, she was,' he finished with relish in his voice.

'Whose dog was that?' I asked.

'She nivver said.'

If I stayed any longer I would lose my temper and do something rash. June would have walked steadily at heel but, just to make sure that Williamson would have no excuse to feel provoked, I put her on the thin lead that I always carry in my pocket. He shouted something after me but I made a point of letting him see that I preferred talking to the dog.

⋆   ⋆   ⋆

Audrey, who had been busily engaged in her favourite task, hosing down the concrete of the runs, finished coiling away the hose and approached.

'I have Mr Branch's dog here,' I told her.

'She was on the farmland, looking for her master. Would you take her back to Mrs Branch and warn her that June may get shot if she gets away again and goes among the sheep?'

'Of course. But first, do you think I could have a minute to tell you something?' she asked shyly.

'If you ask nicely,' I said.

Audrey usually responded to a little leg-pulling in kind, even flirtatiously, but this, it seemed, was not the moment for levity. She pursed her lips. 'Please. Can we go somewhere the others won't see us?'

Between the kennels and the oak trees there are a bench and a table, each cut by chainsaw out of a solid log from the original third oak which had come down in another storm years before. Its successor was only now beginning to contribute its share to the shade and shelter. The surface of the bench had dried enough to be sat on. We could see across the fields to the village and beyond but the house and kennels were hidden by the hedge which we had planted to shelter the dogs from the wind. June lay at our feet, shivering from time to time despite the warmth of the day. I hoped that she had not done herself an injury. She was too old a dog to be tearing across the fields like a lurcher.

110

'Now,' I said. 'What is it?'

Audrey looked at me with large eyes. Her clothes, which belonged on a scarecrow, were well spattered with mud and water but the bone structure of her face was beginning to emerge from the puppy fat and I thought that she had a sixty-forty chance of turning into a good-looking woman. Her skin was good and her chestnut hair had a natural wave and gloss. I could well understand how Sam had fallen under her spell without his yet quite realizing why. One of these years the glow of romance and then the flare of sex would transform him and his relationship with the rest of the world. I felt a momentary stab of pity mingled with envy.

'I wanted Sam to speak to you,' she said, 'but he wanted me to do it because I'm older than he is. And I think it upset him and he wasn't sure that he could keep his voice steady. If I tell you some things, you won't let the others know that it came from me?'

If I had thought of making a funny answer, the seriousness of her expression would have stopped me. 'Definitely not.'

'I wouldn't want Dennis or my auntie to know that I'd made any trouble. We did a lot of switching around, because what one person will tell to another they might not tell somebody else. So while Dennis went with

Francis to see Mrs Jordan, Sam and I went to Mrs Dalton. She's my aunt,' Audrey explained earnestly. 'We made the excuse that we wanted to play a game on Steven's computer. Steven always lets us.

'Aunt Beattie — that's short for Beatrice — was having coffee with Mrs Pelmann on the terrace. Patio, they call it, but that's just being snobs,' Audrey said with serene superiority. 'Anyway, the computer was just inside the window and we could hear every word. *Almost* every word.

'They were talking about Mrs Horner. Well, of course they were. It's the first thing anyone talks about just now.

'They both agreed that she was an awful woman. And I must say that I go along with that,' Audrey said. 'She was the sort of woman who tried to catch you doing something she could complain about. Mrs Bullerton caught Francis smoking once but it was Mrs Horner who phoned his parents. Anyway, Mrs Pelmann said, 'Did you have trouble with her also?' and Aunt Beattie said, 'Who didn't? How do you mean, also? Did she fall out with you too?'

''Did she ever!' Mrs Pelmann said, sounding quite upset. She said that when the McIntoshes are going away they sometimes ask the Pelmanns to look after their house, feed and water their rabbit in the garden and also water the tomatoes in the greenhouse. She said she'd usually let Horace — that's the rabbit, a great big black one — out for a run around. He's very friendly and trusting and never goes far and the garden's well fenced, and anyway he always comes when he's called. He's been neutered,' Audrey explained. 'He's Katherine's rabbit. She's only six and she dotes on him.

'One day early last week, Mrs Pelmann said, she let Horace out while she changed his bedding, and watered and fed Mrs McIntosh's tomatoes. When she'd finished, she couldn't see Horace but he sometimes goes round into the front garden. She went round the house but she couldn't see him there so she walked a little bit along the road calling and came back. Then she found that although there's a solid wall between the two gardens there was a hole where a drain or something went through once upon a time just below ground level, and Horace must have known about it because he'd dug down and gone through to Mrs Horner's garden. She went round to fetch him and Mrs Horner came out and kicked up an awful fuss. She blamed Horace for eating the carnations in her front garden, the bit that's outside the wall, although Horace hadn't been in the front garden and everybody knows it's the wild rabbits from the Moss and Horace could never have eaten that much anyway.' Audrey paused for breath. 'And she said that if it happened again she'd kill and eat him, which was what rabbits were meant for anyway.'

'Not very neighbourly,' I said, 'but not enough to kill for.'

'But there's more,' Audrey said unhappily. 'We couldn't hear very well because she lowered her voice, but something happened on Friday morning. I'm not sure what, but Horace hasn't been in his hutch since then. And Aunt Beattie said something about a replacement and not being able to find something as big and black and friendly. Sam thinks that Mrs Horner must have killed Horace and eaten him and that's what upset him. Would anybody really do something like that?'

'I don't know,' I said. 'But a wise man once said that there's no deed so evil that you can be sure that nobody's ever done it.'

'What I wanted to ask you, Mr Cunningham, was do I tell the police? I don't want to get Mrs Pelmann or anybody else into trouble but I really *like* Mr Branch. When I fell off Sam's bike and cut my knee, he washed the blood off and carried me all the way home.'

I thought it over while she watched me

114

anxiously. 'You've told me,' I said at last. 'That's enough for the moment. I'll tell Mr Hastie what you overheard but not who told it to me. He can tell the police in his own way and time if he finds that he needs to in order to get Mr Branch out of trouble.'

Audrey threw me a relieved smile, jumped to her feet and picked up June's lead. 'Another thing,' I said. 'Do you know who around here received a summons because their dog bit Mrs Horner?'

'I'll see if I can find out.' She turned away.

I called after her, 'Audrey, would you make sure that somebody goes to see Mrs Branch and takes June for walks every day?'

'We're already *doing* that,' she retorted indignantly. 'Dennis went before breakfast but she'd already gone off when Mrs Branch let her out to do a pee in the garden.'

I hurried back to the house. Beth was alone in the kitchen, preparing salad. 'You wouldn't happen to know if anybody around here got a summons because their dog bit Mrs Horner?' I asked.

She shook her head. 'It would have been worth a fine,' she said.

'It might not just be a fine. One or two sheriffs have started ordering the putting-down of dogs that haven't even bitten anybody. Let me know if you hear anything.

I've just about caught up with myself,' I told her. 'I think I'll go and see if I can help your cousin. He'll be at Mrs Horner's house?'

She looked at me in surprise. 'He may be, if he isn't visiting Alistair or arguing with the police. How do you think you can help?'

It was usually easier to tell Beth everything than to try to keep anything from her. The place seemed to be unusually lacking in listening ears. 'Keep it under your hat,' I said, 'or whatever else you happen to be wearing, but I've just heard that there was a row between Mrs Horner and the lady who was to feed the McIntoshes' rabbit while they're away — '

'Mrs Pelmann,' she said.

'How on earth did you know that?'

'Emily McIntosh brought Angus, their West Highland terrier, to board with us while they're away. When she booked him in, she asked if we could keep the rabbit as well. I explained that he wasn't quite the type to be happy in the rabbit pen and he wouldn't take kindly to being stalked by spaniels and pointed by a GSP; and we don't have any other rabbit accommodation. When she brought Angus in, the day before they went off to France, she said that they'd solved the problem of Horace. Mrs Pelmann was going to feed him as she'd done once or twice before.'

Beth sometimes seems to be psychic but there is usually a perfectly logical explanation. 'As simple as that!' I said. 'Apparently, Mrs Horner threatened to kill the rabbit if he came near her garden again and there seems to be some reason to believe that she may have done it. I thought that I might take one of the dogs and see if I can't find some sort of evidence. Bruce may be able to use it to distract attention from Alistair.'

Beth surprised me by nodding cheerfully. 'Take Jason with you. He has the best nose of the lot and he needs the exercise. And I won't say a word.'

'The rain will have washed the scent away.'

'Maybe not. And he could still find a buried rabbit.'

Jason was Beth's personal Labrador. He was getting on in years, rather stiff and slightly grizzled, but Beth was right. He had the best nose in the business and was fixated on rabbits. He could probably find a dead and buried rabbit if it was ten feet down. Jason was enjoying the sun on the front lawn and indulgently watching Sam and Dennis throwing rubber balls for pups to retrieve.

I went indoors for the miniature camera which we use to record the progress of dogs in training, mainly for the benefit of future purchasers. Then I whistled Jason up and took him first to the rabbit pen so that the scent of rabbit would be fresh in his mind. Then we set off by my favourite path. Jason managed a frisk or two and investigated a few patches of cover along the way. If I had been carrying a gun he would have recovered his lost youth and energy for a few hours even if he had suffered for it later.

We emerged beside the pub. I called Jason strictly to heel. As we crossed the bridge over the burn I saw that Bruce had been right. Trees, now in full leaf, on the sloping ground rising from the burn and also above the garden walls of Roland Bovis's and Mrs Horner's houses, cut off the view of all but glimpses of rooftop.

The garden walls of the first house presented a blank face broken only by Bovis's side gate. A strip of front garden between Mrs Horner's house and the road showed definite signs of rabbit damage and I noticed that Jason was showing interest, but the house itself was set into another high garden wall, closed by a pair of wooden gates in need of paint at one gable. There was no room beneath for a rabbit to pass.

I opened half of the gate and confirmed that the water butt only came into view after the first couple of paces, from behind the garage and a Lawson's cypress. The garden was well if unimaginatively kept but the exterior of the house itself was beginning to show signs that expenditure on maintenance was due. We emerged from the gateway again and went to the front door.

Bruce, clipboard in hand, opened the door and beckoned me inside. 'Come on in. I was just about to make coffee.' It was a not displeasing echo of Judith Tolliver. Bruce led the way through a tired-looking hallway to a cramped kitchen and indicated a chair at a plastic-topped table. Jason settled beside me with his chin on my foot. The kettle was coming to the boil.

'Any news of Alistair? Or Mrs Branch?' I asked.

'He's taking it phlegmatically. He has a proper faith in British justice and the Scottish legal system. She's bearing up somehow. The sister who's come to stay with her proves to be a tower of strength. There's not much I can do for either of them at the moment, so I'm getting on with the preliminaries of executry. The only fresh news I can offer you is that I caught up with the lorry driver.'

'The one from the sand-pit?'

'That's the one. He asked me how the hell I expected him to remember anyone that he'd seen from his cab while following a twisting road and approaching a junction and then described a man who was looking down over the rough ground opposite the houses, close to the junction with the main street. Not much of a description, unfortunately, but understandable in the circumstances. The main feature was that he was wearing long, baggy shorts. The driver didn't notice any more, he was too taken up with the man's pale legs.'

'So now all we have to do — ' I began.

'Don't say it! The driver also said that he'd passed a woman walking from the houses towards the sand-pit. He's seen her before, he said. Tall, strong-looking and grey-haired was about all that he could remember.' Bruce slapped his hand down on the desk, sending several papers fluttering to the floor. 'This is the ultimate in awful tasks,' he said peevishly. He looked up at the ceiling and blew out a long breath. 'I don't think that she threw away a piece of paper in her life, her filing system was modelled on a rubbish tip and every scrap has to be scrutinized in case she left a later will or wrote a codicil, or in case there's some clue to an undiscovered fortune. And the worst of it is that the firm doesn't get paid for my work as executor.'

'They don't?' I said. I was under the impression that lawyers were invariably first in the queue for payment.

'When a client asks a solicitor to act as executor, you're more or less bound to accept although it's usually unpaid. Work done as a solicitor can be charged for, but not work as executor. It's a fine dividing line. Provision for a fee can be made in the will but it's a subject that one can hardly bring up at the time, especially if the client isn't all that well off. The most that one can do is to put a little extra onto the account for drawing up the will.'

'And enjoy the client's coffee after she's gone,' I said as he came back to the table with two steaming mugs.

'There is that, although it's only instant and decaff. And then there's the interruptions. I've just had her nephew and his lady-love here.'

'Mrs Bovis?' I said. 'They took their time.'

'They were sailing in the Adriatic and only just got word. They wanted to know all about everything. Fair enough, I suppose, but I could have done without the distraction.'

'I'll go away, if you like.'

'Don't be silly. I don't know what you're doing here, but I'm glad to see you. You can give me a hand with the inventory.'

I have always hated anything that smacks of stock-taking. In the army, I had been known to volunteer for almost anything rather than check stores. 'I can be more helpful than that,' I said hastily. 'I have some fresh information for you. I hear that Mrs Horner was bitten by somebody's dog and was making a fuss about it. If she was pushing for the dog's destruction, that could give the owner a motive. I wouldn't expect the prosecution to go ahead without the principal witness. Can you find out who the owner is?'

'I can try,' he said, 'but it isn't on the public record until it comes to court. The police may tell me, as a favour, but more likely not.'

'Try,' I said. 'And there's more. I can't reveal the source but it should be easy to confirm.' And I told him the tale of the friendly but footloose Horace.

'A little girl's pet rabbit,' he said musingly, 'and it disappears while she's away on holiday. The persons responsible for looking after it would feel very guilty and in my experience one guilt soon spawns another. If there were any suspicion, let alone proof, of . . . What would one call it?'

'Bunnicide,' I suggested.

'Yes, very funny,' he said, po-faced. 'Whatever the real facts, the revelation of other parties with motive and opportunity can be a useful tactic. Unfortunately, one can't spring it on the prosecution. Advance

122

notice has to be given of a defence by impeachment.'

'Hold your horses,' I said. 'It may really have happened that way. If we could prove it, Alistair's off the hook straight away. If Mrs Horner really did snuff poor Horace, what do you suppose happened to the body?'

'I thought you were suggesting that she ate it.'

'She wouldn't have eaten the bones and the pelt, or the contents of the paunch. Would the police tell you what was in her dustbin?'

'As a matter of fact, yes. I asked the question as a matter of routine and was surprised to get an answer. The bins had been emptied on the Thursday and her bin was still empty on the Saturday except for a newspaper, eggshells, one vodka bottle and some cabbage leaves. The refuse bag under her sink held only an empty cat food tin and some potato peelings. A very frugal lady, my late client.'

'Then, assuming that the vicious deed wasn't completed prior to the Thursday, whatever remains of Horace is probably buried in the garden. She wouldn't want to leave it in her dustbin for several days while she could expect the Pelmanns to go on the warpath on behalf of the absent McIntoshes. She may have courted unpopularity, even suspicion, but not universal condemnation, which is what she would have undergone if there had been proof of her eating Katie McIntosh's ewe lamb.'

'You have a point,' Bruce said. 'Let's go and take a look. If it happened that way, I only hope that last night's storm didn't obliterate the last traces.'

'That's what this chap's along for,' I said, indicating Jason. He caught the movement and thumped his tail.

4

Bruce looked from me to the elderly Labrador and then shrugged. 'I suppose we have to accept what help we can get. Give me a minute to tidy up what I've done so far and I'll be with you. Meanwhile — ' he looked at me guilelessly, as lawyers do when they're pulling a fast one ' — you could make a start on the inventory.'

'Not now,' I said. 'Some other year.'

I was becoming mildly curious about the late Mrs Horner and decided to take a look around. The rooms were smaller than I had expected. The furniture was mostly antique but only just qualified for that description and, to my inexpert eye, probably genuine but not of a good period. The pictures were Victorian, oils heavily varnished and darkened with age, sentimental subjects predominating, in gilt frames. In the dining room a pair of glass cupboards displayed some china, not quite down to the category of A Present From Clacton but nothing that struck me as being valuable or even desirable. The carpets and curtains had been good but were now badly worn. Mrs Horner's catering must indeed have been superb if her guests kept returning to the gloomy surroundings.

I heard footsteps outside on the gravel but nobody came to the door. I could see Bruce at a shoddy, folding desk in the sitting room, clipping bundles of paper together. He had the conviction, common in doctors and lawyers, that other people's time came free. I decided to go out and investigate.

There was no one outside at the front of the house but when I walked round through the gate I saw the heavy figure of Sergeant Morrison. He was standing near the greenhouse and looking around him. Beyond the gravel drive, a neatly mown grass path led between strips of delphiniums edging tidy vegetable beds. Mrs Horner had had green fingers and a capacity for hard work in the garden had substituted for expenditure on the house. Her cabbages and lettuces were large and perfectly formed, her onions stood to attention in ranks like soldiers. To judge from the feathered greenery, her carrots would have been perfection. Obviously, no caterpillar or carrot-fly had dared to invade the jealously defended garden.

Keeping Jason strictly to heel I joined the Sergeant on a square of turf under the big pear tree and greeted him by name. 'Are you looking for something in particular?' I asked him.

He shook his head as though scaring away a persistent fly. 'What might you be doing here, Captain Cunningham?' He asked.

'Mister Cunningham, if you don't mind. I came to see Mr Hastie,' I said. In point of fact, it was none of his business what I was doing there now that the police had vacated the place, unless he suspected that I was planning to steal Mrs Horner's tawdry possessions, but my mind had, for once, slipped into gear. 'Tell me, isn't it rather unusual for the local Bobby to be dogsbodying for the officer in charge of a case?'

The Sergeant looked at me in mild surprise but decided to return a civil answer. Bearing in mind the possibility of other ears behind the garden walls I had lowered my voice and he replied in kind. 'Mr Blosson had a CID sergeant with him. It's just he finds he gets more done if he can send his own sergeant out making enquiries and taking statements while he makes use of the local man as a witness and a note taker. That's what he said.'

'And, now that it's a murder case, is Detective Inspector Blosson still in charge of it?'

Sergeant Morrison hesitated. 'Well, now. It only became a case of murder when Mr

Blosson arrested Mr Branch. Until then, it was only a suspicious death, possibly an accident. Detective Superintendent Fraser is in overall charge. But an arrest's been made now, so he's leaving Mr Blosson to tie up the evidence.'

'And is that why you're here?'

'More or less,' he said. The vagueness of the answer was itself very informative.

'You're not quite happy with it,' I suggested.

He drew in his breath sharply, looked around to be sure that DI Blosson was not eavesdropping from behind the cypress tree and lowered his voice further. 'Between ourselves, in confidence?'

'Definitely.'

'If you quote me, I'll deny it.'

'I understand.'

He hesitated again and then it came with a rush. 'No. I'm far frae happy,' he said. 'I ken Mr Branch fine and I canna see him being violent to a woman. My good lady fell and broke her wrist and Mr Branch put her into his car and took her to the hospital, as gently as if she'd been one of his own family. But for some daft reason, Mr Blosson seems to have his knife into him. The evidence against him might convince a jury but it doesna convince me.'

'And having made the arrest and covered himself with glory, Detective Inspector Blosson will not look favourably on any contrary evidence,' I suggested.

'I would not say that at all.' I had gone too far. The Sergeant was constrained by loyalty and I respected him for it. All the same, he was not going to get away with it too easily.

'Has he ever met Mr Branch before now?' I asked.

The Sergeant twitched. 'How would I be knowing a thing like that, now?'

The army had taught me to recognize when a man is being evasive. Pressure now would only push him into a more entrenched position. I filed that subject away for later. 'This Detective Superintendent Fraser,' I said. 'Is he a stocky man, an inch or two shorter than I am? Ginger hair and freckles?'

'Aye. That's the man.'

'I met him when he was a chief inspector. A sound man.'

'He is that.'

My mind was still rushing ahead but, before I could cast out any more lures, Bruce came out of the back door of the house. 'I was just about to tell the Sergeant,' I explained to Bruce, 'that we're going to look for more evidence. I think that he should be with us. An unbiased and official witness to whatever we can find might make the difference between acceptance and the suggestion that we fabricated it. And we can trust him to be honest. We needn't tell him what we're looking for unless we find it.'

Bruce looked searchingly from one to the other of us, but in the end he only said, 'Very well.'

'Let me take this in my own sequence,' I said. 'Come with me. I'll explain later when my mind clears.'

First, I looked at the water butt and the spreading tree — now laden with unripe pears, some of which had fallen in the storm. I checked Jason, who has a habit of eating unripe fruit and then worrying Beth by suffering major stomach upsets. The tree must have been a magnificent sight, I thought, at blossom time but there was little else to be learned. The ground had been trodden over too often, the grass scarred by too many feet, and the water butt had been emptied. I led them instead to the gate in the back wall beside the greenhouse and examined the bolt.

'Did the police open this gate?' I asked the Sergeant.

'Not to my knowledge, and I was here most of the time. Why would we? We were more concerned with keeping nosey Parkers out.

Nobody could have let himself in from outside with the gate bolted as it is.'

'Mr Branch said that he'd never seen it open but it's been opened recently.' I showed them a thin line of bright metal where the rust of ages had been scraped away. My miniature camera could focus down to a very close-up shot and I recorded the signs as best I could. The subject might be too small to register well without a special lens but at least there were witnesses. Unless some policeman owned up to having opened the gate, somebody had gone out that way and, presumably, returned.

'You could have pulled that bolt,' the Sergeant remarked. It was not an accusation but a simple statement of fact. A competent defence counsel would no doubt make the same point in court and I should be warned.

'I could,' I said. 'But I didn't.'

The gate had dropped slightly over the years and to draw the bolt back was a wrestling match. The gate opened with a loud squeak from dry hinges. I caught Bruce's eye. Somebody would have to ask another question of the Pelmanns.

When we emerged into the back lane, the remainder of the layout was immediately clear. There was no fence, the lane being part of the field. A thin strip of grass and clover, with a single surprised-looking holly tree almost opposite the gate, separated the lane from the dark green crop of oilseed rape. The rape had suffered in the storm and already wood pigeon were flighting into the laid patches. To our right, we were looking at the back walls of Roland Bovis's house and garden. The lane continued to the village street through a gate between Roland Bovis's high garden wall and the fence and hedge of the neighbouring cottage. To our left, the lane curved right-handed past the back gardens until it made a sudden turn around the end of the last house and emerged into Old Ford Road. The houses and their gardens were partially screened by the ever-present trees.

I took a careful look at the rough strip between the lane and the field, confining my search to an area corresponding to Mrs Horner's garden. If somebody had come out of the gate to lift a cigar butt and a dog-turd, they would have tried to avoid going far enough along the lane to be seen and remembered. But if there had ever been any signs left, time and the storm had obliterated them, or else I was too incompetent to find them. Jason joined me by sniffing along the rough fringe, investigating the visits of other dogs, but I could see from his body language that there was no trace of rabbit or game.

There were one or two old dog droppings in the grass but that was to be expected. Nobody picks up faeces on farmland. I took a few photographs to illustrate the layout and left it at that.

We returned to the garden and I bolted the gate behind us. My mind had gone into overdrive. 'Could you get us a sample of the famous dog-plonk?' I asked the Sergeant.

'I doubt that,' he said. 'It'll be stored at the police lab.'

'How about a close-up photograph of it?'

He nodded. 'I could maybe manage that. Mr Blosson had extra copies made.' The Sergeant did not ask why I wanted them. Either he was singularly incurious or he was thinking along much the same lines as I was. I thought it better not to probe.

'Was any search made in the garden for disturbed ground?' I asked.

'The lady had been gardening,' the Sergeant replied.

'In fancy earrings?' Bruce said doubtfully.

Sergeant Morrison shrugged. 'There was only the hoe taken out and a watering can. She was wearing heavy shoes, only fit for the garden. My guess is that she'd changed her shoes and that was all she needed to change. She likely planned to do a few minutes of light gardening, just tidying up and watering the greenhouse plants, before she put on fancier shoes and went out to the shops or suchlike.'

If Mrs Horner had been using a hoe, it was unlikely that any signs remained of a burial several days earlier. I let Jason try his nose. His walk changed and he made small noises in his throat. I knew his language well. It was evident that there had been at least one rabbit in the garden. He followed a scent-trail which zigzagged into the corner between the greenhouse and the garden wall, then turned and retraced his steps. He was hesitant and not showing his usual interest and I could tell that the trail was an old one.

I cast him out again but it was evident that the rain had washed any scent away except where the ground was sheltered by the pear tree. Nevertheless, I kept him working and, obliging as ever, he quartered the ground, taking his own time.

Jason began to show interest again in the middle of the row of delphiniums that had been planted to make a partial screen to the larger vegetable patch. One clump, still showing flowers of that remarkable blue, seemed to be wilting despite the night's rain. When Jason came to that place he slowed, pointed and then began to scratch around the plant.

134

I called him away and photographed the place. 'Is there a spade?' I asked.

'You think there's something buried there?' the Sergeant asked.

'The dog certainly does,' I said. 'And he's not often wrong.'

'Her spade's in the greenhouse, but you'd best not touch it. There's a wee shovel in the coalhouse. Bide a moment while I fetch it.'

He was back with the small shovel in seconds. We examined it together but there was no sign that it had been used for anything but coal. It was not an ideal tool but it would serve. It seemed to be agreed that the Sergeant should do any digging. I photographed him at work.

The clump of delphiniums came up easily. It had recently been lifted and replanted. A few inches deeper, the shovel hit something soft. After a few moments of trial and error the Sergeant uncovered and lifted out onto the grass path a skin covered in muddy black fur, an assortment of rabbit bones and a set of guts.

I called away Jason, who was becoming very interested in the bones and guts. 'One more moment before we explain,' I said. I led them, firmly including Jason, back to the corner by the greenhouse. A short rake was standing in the corner between the door and the wall. Its wooden handle was too rough to take fingerprints but I used my clean handkerchief to lift it carefully. Several fine black hairs still clung to the metal tines and there was a trace of blood.

Poor Horace. Poor Katie.

'Mr and Mrs Pelmann can give you the details,' I said, 'but here's an outline.' I explained to the Sergeant about Mrs Horner's earlier threat to kill and eat Horace if he invaded her garden again. 'You can see clearly what happened,' I said. 'Horace did come under the wall again, attracted by all these vegetables. Mrs Horner will have filled the hole in later. She chased him around the garden and cornered him beside the green-house. It wouldn't be much of a chase — I'm told that he was a very friendly and trusting rabbit. She used the rake to kill him. And then she ate him.'

'A little girl's rabbit?' We had lowered our voices further so that the Sergeant spoke barely above a whisper but his professional impassivity had gone and I could hear and understand the revulsion in his voice. A child's pet and the eating of meat were too far apart to be thought of together.

'A little girl's rabbit. Mrs Horner was just that sort of person, cruel and sly. She buried the remainder rather than leave it in her bin, in case anyone insisted on looking in it.'

The Sergeant had produced his pocket-book and was writing busily. 'I'd met the woman, of course,' he said. 'She was aye one to complain and she'd no hesitation about having a neighbour — '

He broke off.

'Prosecuted?'

'Maybe.'

'Who?' I asked.

'I can't tell you that.' Clearly he was under direct orders.

'Let it go,' Bruce said. 'I may be able to find out through the fiscal's office.'

The Sergeant took refuge in his notes. 'Just so's I understand, the rabbit belonged to the McIntosh lassie next door, but they're abroad just now and the rabbit was being looked after by Mrs Pelmann. Is that the way of it?'

'So we believe,' Bruce said. 'Can you think of anything more certain to generate friction?'

'Yes,' the Sergeant and I said in unison. His face shifted for an instant towards the other houses strung out along Old Ford Road. I believe that we were both thinking of a death threat, via a prosecution in court, against a beloved dog.

'The more important question,' said Bruce, 'is where do we go from here? You're a witness to what we've found?'

'That I am,' the Sergeant said stoutly. 'There can be no denying it.'

'But would you like to go further and take the credit for these discoveries?'

The Sergeant reared back like a startled horse. 'Here! There's no way I'm making out that I went investigating behind the back of a superior officer, contradicting his findings. I'd be way out of line.'

'Properly speaking,' said Bruce to me, 'we should let the Sergeant make whatever report he thinks fit. Nearer the time for the trial, we would produce our evidence and, if we're quite sure who the other culprit would be, make our plea of impeachment. The trouble with that is that Mr Branch would have to spend months on remand and in custody. And he's not a young man any more. The days and weeks and months will be precious to him.'

'That's not the only disadvantage,' I said. 'It would mean that the police spend the intervening period bolstering the case against Alistair and picking holes in this alternative or at the very least investigating it with lukewarm enthusiasm. Tell me, is DI Blosson the golden boy as far as Detective Superintendent Fraser's concerned?'

During the slur which I had cast on police impartiality, the Sergeant had made a show of his mind being elsewhere. He returned his overt attention to me. 'I wouldn't say quite that.' His voice became almost inaudible. Divided loyalties were pulling him apart. 'Mr Fraser has been heard to say that the DI's getting too big for his boots, so I've been told.'

I looked at Bruce. 'It seems to me that you must seek an interview with the Detective Superintendent. You'd better get my film developed first. Meanwhile, we must bag the bits of rabbit for the Sergeant to keep safe. Strictly speaking the guts should go into a nylon bag, because there are traces of other chemicals which come out of polythene, but polythene will have to do. Did Mrs Horner leave any freezer bags?'

'I think so.' Bruce turned, stopped and said a mildly rude word. I said a worse one. Only the Sergeant confined himself to an outburst of tongue clicking.

Jason had broken away from heel. I photographed him as he was consuming the last of the rabbit guts.

* * *

I headed towards home. Jason, well aware that he was in disgrace, stayed very close to heel.

Isobel, Beth and Hannah were already at lunch under the silver birch when I arrived. I had promised Audrey that I would not name her as my informant, but the morning's discoveries were another matter. I told them my tale, but very much in confidence, without mentioning my original source. I also described, in some detail, Jason's fall from grace. I sensed some amusement emanating from Hannah and Isobel, but Beth, already justly indignant at the tale of Horace's killing, was very much incensed. Jason, conscious that he had sinned and was under discussion, hid under an escallonia bush and refused to come out.

It was time to catch up with work. In parallel with the confusingly nicknamed You, Sid (short for Cedar) would be one of our first entrants in the competitions in the coming season and, provided that he attained Field Trial Champion status, was a major hope for both breeding stock and stud fees in the years to come. He was a promising, not to say brilliant, performer but almost over-eager and so sometimes given to signs of unsteadiness. I decided to concentrate on him for a while in the real world as opposed to the artificial world of dummy training. I fetched my gun, some cartridges, a game bag and Sid. Now that the sultry heat had moderated, the

Moss would not be the humid and midge-ridden hell of the previous fortnight. We set off on foot.

It seemed that Sid had suddenly matured or else had benefited greatly from a series of lessons in the wood with a dummy covered in rabbit skin fired from the launcher or pulled suddenly across his path by catapult rubber and a remote release. I had managed at last to rid him of the notion that he was ever free to make his own decisions or could disobey without bringing about his ears the wrath of his handler. The Moss was hopping with rabbits and Sid worked a perfect pattern, sending them out of the thicker cover. Sometimes I had to hold my hand because I could not be sure that neither Sid nor any courting couple was in the background; and I was waiting for a three-quarter-grown rabbit to show. A full-grown rabbit in midsummer may be a doe still feeding a litter and I always try to avoid leaving young creatures to starve underground.

Sid had learned at last to harass rabbits in the bushes but to halt as soon as they bolted from cover. I checked him once for a mild error and he settled down. Working him became as easy as moving my own hand. When at last I had a chance of the rabbit I wanted and bowled it over in the open, Sid took a pace in its direction and then, remembering his lessons, stopped and sat. I shook a finger at him, which was usually enough of a reproof. The rabbit was motionless. A young dog can be put off retrieving by a struggling and resentful bird or rabbit. I counted slowly to ten and then sent him for the retrieve. He delivered it to my hand almost daintily.

Somebody else was shooting on the Moss. I could hear shots coming from the direction of the small loch, usually two shots followed by an interval of variable length. Either some-body was in trouble — two shots, repeated, is a general signal of distress — or he was shooting pigeon, taking a right-and-left and then waiting until the birds regained their confidence and returned. The sound of the shots was soft, which gave me a clue to the shooter's identity. I walked in that direction, letting Sid hunt but still ready to correct the least unsteadiness. He behaved perfectly and he knew it. He was taking pride at last in doing it right. I began to have hopes for the coming season and pity for any man who had never known the euphoria of working as a team with a favourite dog.

The loch had been at a low level until the previous night's rain. There was no feeder stream and yet, as if magically, the water had been replenished from an underwater spring and was back at its usual height. Not far from the new brink, a pair of large, upturned tree roots made the basis of a serviceable hide. I had made use of it myself on occasions, usually when duck were flighting in. A man was seated under a scrap of camouflage net, waiting for the pigeon to return for a drink. He was wearing ear protectors which had prevented him hearing my approach, but his spaniel nudged his arm and he looked round. I recognized Bob Guidman from the village, a round-faced, broad-spoken, smiling man of middle age who was supplementing his redundancy money by shooting pigeon and rabbits and selling them to the game dealer. He also managed to persuade several of the local farmers into contributing, in the interest of crop protection, the cost of twelve-bore cartridges, turning another profit by lightly loading his own cartridges in the much smaller twenty-eight-bore and pocketing the considerable saving. In his hands the very small but tightly choked gun was an effective killer at moderate range. Half a dozen shot pigeon had been arranged in natural attitudes at the water's edge.

'It's you, Captain,' he informed me. He was one of the few people I allowed to address me by my army rank, and I never knew why I indulged him. 'Come to join me?' He pushed his ear protectors up.

'I'll sit with you for a minute, Bob,' I said. 'I won't shoot.'

Bob's spaniel, Moss, had been bought from me as a pup while Bob was still earning good money as an offshore welder. Moss and Sid were distantly related and knew each other well. They lay down together. I ducked under the net and seated myself on a grassy shelf. There was a small stack of plastic pigeon decoys beside Bob's feet. These would have attracted the first comers and been replaced as soon as dead birds were available. More shot birds were laid in the shade to cool.

I wanted to lead into the subject of Mrs Horner's death, but the native Fifer is inclined to recoil if approached too directly. Like Beth, I prepared to work round to it obliquely. 'I thought you'd be decoying over the rape today,' I said.

He shook his head. 'There's laid patches a over; and it's nae handie tae mak decoys show ower rape. The buggers can tak a feed oniewhere, but they aye hae to come for a drink. I'll wait for the rape stubble at the back o my hoose, efter it's cut.'

I nearly missed the mention but something rang a little bell in my mind. 'Where exactly do you live, Bob?' I asked.

'In the main street. The wee hoose next to Mr Bovis.'

Knowing those cottages, the kitchen would almost certainly be at the back. It was a bonus but I decided to leave it for the moment. 'Was there water in the lochan on Saturday?' I asked.

'Some.'

'You were here, then?'

'Aye. In the morning.'

'You know what happened?'

'M'hm. Whisht, now.'

We waited. I sat very still, watching through the net. Movement is the give-away. I was looking towards Old Ford Road, perhaps a quarter of a mile distant. A small group of four or five wood pigeon headed for the pool. For a moment they looked like settling on the far side of the water, out of shot, but they saw the decoy birds and swung round. I half expected Bob to let them land and take them on the ground, but he was more of a sportsman than that. As they were dropping he took a right and left. The small and lightly loaded gun made little noise but the two birds fell, leaving pale feathers floating in the air, while their fellows headed for the horizon. One bird was dead, lying in a natural position, breast down. Bob sent his spaniel for the other. Moss was wise enough to go for the one that still had a flutter left, ignoring the others. The bird had died by the time he returned with it.

We settled again. Bob reloaded from a pocket.

'I ken fine what happened,' Bob said, as though there had been no interruption. 'Somebody droondit Mrs Horner in her ain water butt. Aboot bloody time, an a.'

'You fell out with her?'

A ferocious scowl sat uneasily on his usually smiling face. 'No tae say fell oot. She aimed a kick at Moss, one time. I telled her that if the kick had landed I'd've tugged her heid aff and stuffed it up her erse. She set up a squawk but she never tried it again. You're nae thinking that I droondit the auld biddy like a kitten?'

'Did you?'

He shook his head — regretfully, I thought.

'No, I wasn't thinking that,' I told him. 'You know that they're holding Mr Branch for it?'

'Aye. Damn shame. He's proper gentleman, Mr Branch, and no even ane tae haud the gullie ower the dyke.'

Bob was always broad-spoken but now he was stretching my understanding of idiom in the Scots language to breaking point. 'To stand up for himself, do you mean?'

'Aye. He'd nivver hae said an ill word tae the bitch, let alone laid hand on her.'

Evidently the words *De mortuis nil nisi bonum did* not appear on the Guidman family crest.

'You may be able to help him,' I said. 'You were sitting here. If you were watching for incoming pigeon you'd be looking mostly about the level of the houses in Old Ford Road and any movement would catch your eye. Who did you see come and go?'

A single pigeon came over and in his momentary uncertainty he missed it by about ten feet, behind and below. 'I wouldna want tae drop some laddie in the sharn for daein what I'd've liked fine to dae mysel,' he said at last, 'but if it's for Mr Branch . . . I didna see muckle, mind. Look for yersel. The trees howd the maist o' the hooses.'

That was true, but the trees did not make an impenetrable screen and the road level was visible here and there below the lower branches. 'You can see where people would walk past Mrs Horner's house and the one next to it, the McIntoshes' house.'

'Is that whose it is? I wasna paying muckle heed, mind. But whan I wis just thinking of packing up tae gae hame tae my dinner, my ee was catchit by a man and a wumman, daundering towards the main street. I couldna see fa it

147

was, it's ower far. And a mintie later there was a mannie on his ain went the same wye.'

'What time was that?' I asked him.

'Damned if I ken. Nearing twelve, I'd guess. If it helps, a lorry came by from the quarry just efter.'

'It could help a whole lot. Can you tell me anything at all about those three people?'

'No a damn thing. It's o'er far. See yon mannie?'

I looked. There was a figure at Mrs Horner's gate. I recognized the colour of Bruce's golf jacket. 'That's Mr Hastie,' I said. 'Can you not remember anything about their clothes?'

'See, now. The first twasome, the wumman was in a white dress. Her hair was dark.' Bob closed his eyes in the effort of recall. A dozen pigeon flew over but it would have been the wrong moment to distract him. 'The chiel was wearing dark strides and a light shirt, white or pale colour. The second man had fawn breeks and jacket to match, mebbe a suit. And yon, so help me, is a that I can mind.'

Bob opened his eyes as the pigeon came round again and he was in time to catch up with the last one. The bird turned over in a puff of feathers and dropped well clear of the decoy birds.

'Do you mind if I send Sid for that one?' I asked. 'He needs the practice.'

Bob graciously agreed and Sid went out. I directed him by hand signals onto the pigeon which had fallen into a clump of reeds. He picked up the loose-feathered bird without enthusiasm — many dogs quite reasonably dislike filling their mouths with feathers — but he brought it perfectly to hand. I put it with the others.

'I must go,' I told Bob. 'Have the police asked you about what you've just told me?' He shook his head. I cursed the absent Detective Inspector. It seemed that he had found the evidence that suited his book and then stopped work. 'When you see your wife,' I said, 'would you ask her what she saw from her kitchen window on Saturday morning?'

'Aye, I'll dae that,' Bob said.

I left him crouched in his hide and worked Sid back in the general direction of home. Once I was well clear I could hear the gentle popping of Bob's shotgun as the pigeon trickled in again to drink.

Sid was investigating a clump of gorse, which I knew overlaid a bed of rock so that there were no rabbit holes below, when I heard my name called. I looked over my shoulder to where Allan Carmichael, the photographer, was waiting at a safe distance, his camera at the ready. When I returned my attention to business, I was in time to see six or seven white scuts vanishing down the holes in a bank fifty yards away. Sid emerged from the gorse, sat and looked at me reproachfully. He had done his bit and I had let him down. I called him to heel and sat him again, unloading my gun as Carmichael arrived.

'Am I spoiling something?' he asked anxiously.

'Nothing that mattered,' I said.

'I would have stayed well clear except that I have your prints in my pocket.' He produced an A5 envelope from a capacious inner pocket. We took a seat on an outcrop of the same rock that underlay the gorse. The envelope was packed with glossy prints and as he sifted through them I recognized a succession of local scenes.

He isolated and handed over some excellent shots of the dogs working, some of them including me as a foreground figure. 'These are splendid,' I told him. 'How much do I owe you?'

He waved his hand vaguely. 'Nothing. It was a pleasure.'

I thanked him. 'Could I borrow the whole packet for a day or two?' I asked.

'I don't see why not. But why do you want them?'

'You were trotting to and fro on Saturday morning,' I said. 'You know what happened?'

'You mean about Mrs Horner?'

'Yes. You may have caught something or someone in the background that could be useful.'

He looked concerned. 'Then shouldn't I give them to the police?'

'I think,' I said, 'that it would be perfectly proper for me to show them to Alistair Branch's lawyer and let him decide.'

'In that case, go right ahead,' he said, handing over his envelope. 'I like Mr Branch. I like him a lot.'

★   ★   ★

I would have liked to call in at the hotel on the way home but eyebrows might have been raised if I had walked in with an uncovered shotgun.

Feeding time was still in progress when I reached Three Oaks. (To the relief of Sid, who knew for a fact that he would be forgotten and left to starve if he were not on the spot when food was handed out.) The junior helpers had collected their meagre wages and gone off to spend them. Henry was helping out but, between stiffening joints and a tendency to stop and chat with each

151

dog along the way, his contribution hardly made up for the absence of Daffy.

I lent a hand with the distribution of the dogs' meals and subsequent dish washing, but first I phoned the pub. Mrs Hebden answered. I asked whether she could tell me who had taken lunch there on the Saturday.

'Not for sure,' she said doubtfully. 'Is it important?'

'It is, rather,' I said. 'Mr Branch's lawyer will want to know.'

'I'll do what I can,' she said immediately. 'I feel awful about telling the police all about his spat with Mrs Horner.'

'Somebody else would have told them if you hadn't.'

'It's good of you to say so. We were quite full on Saturday and if strangers called in on the way past we've no way of knowing who they were. I'll check the bookings and ask the waitresses who they can remember and I'll phone or give Mr Kitts a note for you. Will that do?'

'That will do fine,' I said, 'and I'm sure Mr Branch will be grateful.'

I had finished helping out and was heading back to the house for the shower and change which were habitual to me when the physical part of the day's work was over, when Bruce's Vectra turned in at the gate. I tried to escape into the house but he caught me in the hall.

'A word in your ear,' he said.

I sighed. 'If that's where you want to put it,' I said wearily. I had no intention of being kept standing on tired legs in the hall, nor of inviting Bruce into my bathroom with me. I was very dry after my hours in the open air and sunshine so I decided that drinks time had arrived a little earlier than usual and led him into the sitting room. He looked surprised and disapproving when I offered him a drink, but when he heard my beer gurgling into the glass he decided that perhaps, after all, his working day could be considered over. He then went on to prove that it was not.

When he had filled his glass to his satisfaction, he held the cold side against his brow for a moment. I noticed that he was looking a little frayed and shopsoiled. Then he drank and put down the glass.

'Better, now?' I asked.

'A very, very little. I think I've blown it. I tried to phone Superintendent Fraser to make an appointment to go and see him but they just took the phone number for Mrs Horner's house. Somebody called me back on his behalf a few minutes later, which was precisely the courtesy I didn't want. I'd hoped to have a quiet chat with the

Superintendent himself where I could show him your photographs and sound him out. Your photographs came out well, by the way. I paid extra for the one-hour service — you can reimburse me for the shots of dogs carrying things. Anyway, I found myself being asked what I wanted to speak to him about and when I suggested coming to see him they said that he wouldn't trouble me to go all the way to Kirkcaldy. The message wasn't exactly, 'Come to the point or get off the line and don't bug us,' but words to that effect were hanging in the air.

'So I had to do what I least wanted and speak to Fraser over the phone, with God knows who listening in. And he'd already heard about the rabbit skin so I was left with nothing very new to offer except to point out that the case against my client was circumstantial in the extreme, that the only physical evidence could easily have been transplanted, that as good a case could probably have been made against others and that he was holding a very mild-mannered man on the strength of evidence which might just possibly persuade a sheriff to commit him for trial but would certainly not convince a judge and jury. He listened politely and then said that he'd look into the matter and get back to me.'

'And so he probably will.'

'More likely he'll tell Blosson to look again and then pass on his conclusions,' Bruce said.

'No,' I said. 'He's a fair man and a conscientious one.'

'I hope you're right but I'm afraid you're not. I did ask that he give me his answer face-to-face and he didn't exactly promise but I gathered that he would probably come through to see the scene for himself and, if so, he'd meet me there. I asked him to give me at least a few minutes notice so that I could get hold of you.'

'Me? Why me?'

Bruce gave me the sort of look that one might give to a backward child. 'Because you did most of the deducing, searching, finding and listening. And you know the locality and a lot of the people. You could interpret the actions of that damn dog — all but eating the evidence, which even I could understand if not approve. Your account would carry more conviction than mine. So I wanted to ask you to stick around for the next few days where I can find you if I need you in a hurry.'

'I suppose so,' I said. I spent most of my days in or near Three Oaks so that normally it would have been no hardship. 'But I meant to go to Kirkcaldy tomorrow,' I said.

'If you're in luck and I'm not, the Detective Superintendent may invite us to go there for a discussion. Otherwise, I'd rather that you were within reach. You could always help me with the inventory,' he added hopefully, sounding like somebody offering a favour.

'For the same hourly rate that you're being paid?'

'In your dreams! What are friends for?'

'Not for helping you with inventories,' I told him.

*　*　*

Bruce settled down to study some papers and I headed for the stairs again. This time, it was the phone that stopped me. I picked it up in the kitchen and flopped into one of the basket chairs.

'Captain?' said Bob Guidman's voice. 'I did as you winted and spak tae the auld leddy. Saturday forenoon she was watching oot o the kitchen windae, cause I'd axed her to keep an ee on the cushies. If they war feeding at ony yin place in the rape field, I wis going to try my luck there.'

'And?' I said. 'Can I speak to her?'

'Och, she's no liking for a this technology. I'll tell you mysel. She thinks she seen Mr Branch go back alang the lane towards his ain hoose. Aboot half-eleven, that would hae been, or mebbe a bittie earlier.'

'She can't be sure?'

'She says it wis awfie like him an there wis a liver-and-white spaniel. He'd on a fawn blazer and white breeks.'

'Many thanks,' I said. 'If that's what Alistair Branch was wearing on Saturday, she may have done him a big favour.'

'Dinna hing up,' Bob said quickly. 'I've no finished. A minute or twa efter that, a mannie in a white shirt and khaki shorts came out of the back yett tae the auld bitch's hoose. He stooped doon for a while an then gaed back intil her gairden an the yett shut.'

'Who?' I asked. 'Who was it?'

'She couldna tell.'

'A stranger?' I suggested.

'Maybe, but likely no. He was facing the other way, a-purpose, while he could, an keeping yon holly between hissel an these hooses. Could ha been Mr Pelmann, or Roley Bovis from next door, or some other thickset, black-heided chiel of that sort. Mrs Bovis, even, the way she was putting on the beef, last time I seed her.'

'It can't have been Mr Bovis,' I said. 'He was at an auction in Kirkcaldy.' I decided to leave more detailed questioning to the police, but there was one vital question to which I was burning to know the answer. 'Ask her whether there would have been time for Mr Branch to get home after she saw him, change his trousers and get round to Mrs Horner's house?'

'I a'ready axed her that. She said no.'

'She'll say the same to the police?'

'Aye. She will that.'

'Thank you, Bob,' I said. 'And give thanks to your wife. You may be helping to prevent a good man being set up.'

I went back into the sitting room to give Bruce the glad tidings.

'She doesn't seem to be very positive,' he said doubtfully. 'Perhaps I'd better phone and speak to her before I ring the Detective Superintendent.'

'I don't think she approves of telephones,' I told him. 'You'd better go and see her.'

★ ★ ★

This time, I managed to make it all the way upstairs. I came down, feeling much refreshed, to find that Bruce had taken me at my word and gone out, but the rest of the gang had already foregathered in the sitting room and Henry was dispensing my drinks with a generous hand.

As usual, business was cleared away first. While decision-making was rife I brought up the current area of dispute. The diary was beginning to fill with engagements — field trials and invitations to shoot or to pickup, all clashing and competing for attendance. For once, we were more or less unanimous even if some of the decisions were unsatisfactory compromises. I made entries in the firm's diary and hid it away quickly before mind-changing could begin.

Business finished, the questions surrounding the death of Mrs Horner were given an airing. First extracting an oath of confidentiality which had at least a fair chance of being honoured, I brought them up to date with developments, withholding only the source of my information about Mrs Pelmann and the unfortunate Horace.

If the sin of killing and eating a little girl's pet rabbit was already known to them, the retelling of it brought down a fresh wave of condemnation on the late Mrs Horner. Beth's comment was typical: 'I always knew that she was a horrid person,' she said, 'but I wouldn't have believed that anybody could be so beastly. I'm not surprised that she was murdered.'

'Are you suggesting that Mr or Mrs Pelmann, or the two together, killed her?' Henry asked.

'Well, no. Probably not. I was only

suggesting that anybody who could do that sort of thing could do other things even worse, and make serious enemies.'

Henry introduced a fresh slant. 'If your informant quoted the conversation accurately to you and you repeated it verbatim,' he said to me, 'there was at least a suggestion that Mrs Dalton also had had a slanging match with the since deceased lady.'

'I believe you're right,' I said.

'I'm sure you are,' Beth said. 'Months ago, I called at the shop. Mrs Horner was already at the counter and Mrs Dalton followed me in. Mr Campbell was serving and he chatted to both of them and they both chatted back to him but not a word to each other. I thought at the time that there had to be a coldness between them, but Mrs Horner made a hobby of putting folks' backs up so I forgot about it.'

Mention of Mrs Guidman's observations from her kitchen window brought Roland Bovis back to mind. 'When are you going south again?' I asked Henry.

'Late on Sunday,' he said. 'My ward seems to have fallen out with one of the tenant farmers and I'll have to spend a day or two sorting it out.'

'I was going to take a couple of hours off tomorrow and go to Kirkcaldy for that gun,' I told him, 'but now Bruce wants me to stay available.'

'I'll go,' Henry said immediately. 'There's another auction on Saturday and I'd like to look at the pictures.'

'Well, for God's sake don't buy any more,' Isobel said, 'unless you're going to buy me a bigger house.'

5

I found Friday's Scottish papers interesting. When I saw the first editorial — in the *Scotsman* — I walked down to the village. Mrs Campbell allowed me to glance at the others. While still managing to report on developments in the case of Mrs Horner (without actually having anything new to say) each admitted to having been fooled by the lady's letters, which had purported to come from many different members of the public. Acknowledgements ranged from bald admissions to what verged on abject apologies to the whole canine species. What interested me was that the truth had emerged simultaneously in all the papers. Evidently there had been much comparing of notes before the unpalatable truth was accepted.

I met Bruce again outside the front door. 'There was nobody at home at the Guidmans' yesterday,' he said. 'Well, I suppose everybody has to go out some time. I only came back for some papers and I'll try there again later on. Are you coming?'

'I have more than enough to do here,' I told him. 'I was going to take a brace of young dogs for some training on the Moss, but I suppose you want me to be more available than that?'

'Train them here,' he snapped. He had been looking forward to collecting his fiancée to sail on the catamaran which a friend of his kept in Tayport harbour. He cleared his throat and, with an effort, summoned up his reserves of diplomacy. 'I may as well go back to Mrs Horner's house. If Detective Superintendent Fraser's as good as his word and comes to meet me, today or any other day, I want to be there before he changes his mind. And I can't see myself prattling convincingly about scents and rabbits.'

'Your apology is accepted,' I said.

Before he could decide whether or not to deny that any apology had been offered, a dark Isuzu Trooper, clean and shining but beginning to show rust, turned in at the gate and stopped with a yelp of tyres. I turned towards it with my eyebrows raised and what I hoped was a polite and enquiring smile. We still had two trained dogs for sale and we were at the time of year when owners suddenly realize that the old dog is getting too stiff to work for another season.

It was soon clear that this was no prospective client. The sole occupant came out of the car like a bull through a hedge. He was a tall man, almost bald, with a barrel chest, a flat stomach and an athletic step. The fact that he was well into middle age seemed an irrelevance among so much energy. His face, which was heavily modelled, was twisted into an expression of controlled anger. In the bright sunlight it was difficult to make out whether he was snorting steam, but I could well have believed it.

'Which of you is Cunningham?' he demanded.

I was tempted to point at Bruce but honesty prevailed. 'I am.'

He rounded on Bruce. 'Then you're Hastie? The lawyer?' His big hands made a pass in the air.

He thrust forward, almost colliding chest to chest with Bruce. Bruce, showing courage which surprised me, refused to step back. 'Go ahead,' he said. 'Use violence. I haven't had a good lawsuit in weeks. What seems to be your problem?'

The moderate answer took some of the wind out of the big man's sails. 'Seems? Seems?' He found more words and forced them out between gritted teeth. 'My problem, as you call it, is that you two have been suggesting that the Horner woman was killed by me or my wife. We've just had the police at us, asking questions, one after the other. And,

164

I may tell you, I've a lawyer of my own.'

'Factual statements made to the police are not actionable,' Bruce said.

Although we had cast suspicious glances towards several, if not most, of the villagers, there was only one family who could have been advised of it by the police. The man seemed to be building up a second head of steam. 'In point of fact,' I said, 'we never suggested anything of the sort. I take it that you're Mr Pelmann?'

He nodded, the action looking more like an aborted head-butt. I noticed that he was wearing navy slacks and a white shirt open at the neck. He could have been the man who Bob Guidman had seen walking with a woman. 'You admit it then? Or how did you know who I was?'

'Did the police tell you that we had made any such statement?' Bruce enquired. Hannah appeared in the doorway and he called to her. 'Hannah, come and be a witness.'

Hiding a smile, Hannah approached and waited.

'Well?' Bruce said.

Pelmann was deflating. 'They implied it,' he said vaguely. 'Your names were mentioned.'

'That was very indiscreet of them,' I said. 'They may have meant to make mischief. Do you ever wear shorts?' I asked him.

'Good God, no!' Pelmann seemed to be confused by the turns the discussion had taken so that he was relieved to find something to be indignant about. 'I hate to see hairy knees about the place, even my own.'

'You know that they've arrested Alistair Branch, on very slender evidence?' I asked.

'I heard,' he said gruffly. He seemed uncertain whether to continue directing his antagonism at us or to switch it to the police. 'Bloody nonsense. If Alistair sees a beetle in front of him he steps carefully over it. Least violent person I know.'

'I agree,' I told him. 'And all we've done is to point out that there are others with the opportunity and as strong a motive. Yours haven't been and won't be the only names mentioned. Far from it.'

'You think we'd have killed her over somebody else's pet rabbit? Come on! I'll apologize to the McIntoshes when they come back and offer to buy Katie a new rabbit and that will be the end of it. With a little luck, it'll mean that they never ask us to house-sit or rabbit-sit again.'

'It's no less unlikely than killing her over a dogturd,' I said, 'and once the deed was done, anybody would have had a motive to try and shift the blame onto poor Alistair.'

'Well, don't you try to shift it onto either of us.'

'We're not trying to incriminate anybody,' Bruce said. 'But the evidence against Mr Branch is slim and could have been contrived. You're as convinced as we are that he's innocent. The more people we can suggest who had equal motives and opportunities, the sooner the police will have to realize that their case is seriously flawed.'

Pelmann thought that over and I saw his muscles relaxing. 'Damned if that isn't quite reasonable, in a wacky sort of way,' he said at last. 'But, dammit, there must have been dozens of people with that much reason to drown the old bitch. Why pick on me? She was the most malicious bugger I ever came across. Anybody could have done it — *and* got a vote of thanks from the community.'

'It just happened that a member of the police was present when we turned up Horace's pelt and bones,' I said. 'That's the only reason you came to be singled out. You wouldn't care to suggest a few more names to put forward?'

'No, I bloody wouldn't! These are my neighbours. And my friends.'

It seemed to me that while he was in a less aggressive and more confiding mood it might

167

be a chance to gather some more information. 'How about Mrs Dalton?' I suggested.

He froze. I thought for a moment that I had gone too far. Then I saw a gleam of amusement come into his eye. It was followed by a twist to his mouth suggesting that he was not without a trace of the malice which he had attributed to the late Mrs Horner. 'You do get bypassed by the local gossip, don't you?' he said.

'I heard that she had had a major row with Mrs Horner,' I said.

'She and everybody else. Yes, you could put it that way.' He paused again, restraining himself, but malice conquered all. Or perhaps it was the lure of a story to a natural raconteur. He leaned back against his car in the relaxed attitude of a man entertaining friends with anecdotes in the pub. 'I'll tell you a part of it. This was a year or so back. The Daltons had only just moved here and they hardly knew anybody, but Mrs Horner had at least been civil to them. The Daltons were due for a holiday abroad to celebrate a wedding anniversary. When they told the police that the house would be empty, the cops asked who would be holding the key and the Daltons could only think of asking Mrs Horner.

'Well, when they came back they could see

that their things had been disturbed. Mrs Horner had gone through everything. She'd even invited her few cronies to join her.' Pelmann saw my eyebrows go up. 'Hellish thing to do, wasn't it? I don't wonder that you're surprised.'

'I was only surprised that you mentioned friends,' I told him. 'I didn't think that there was any such animal. She seemed to have taken an advanced course in How To Lose Friends And Alienate People.'

'She did have a few. Not many and none of them friendly. She was tolerated rather than liked. Nobody inside the village, she'd alienated all of them except Roland Bovis. For some reason, and I really can't believe that it was sex — although the most extraordinary couples do make music together — the two of them got on like the proverbial house on fire. Martha Bullerton out at Seagrove Cottages, only half a mile away, was quite pally with her, to name another, and one or two ladies in Cupar. If you didn't keep a dog and were prepared to listen to some of her nastiness, she could be quite affable.

'The word didn't take long to go round. Mrs Dalton may look as though butter wouldn't melt in her mouth, or anywhere else for the matter of that. Do you know her?

You'd think that she didn't have a thought in her head beyond darning the minister's socks, collecting for charity and other good works, but she must be a warm piece in secret. By the time the Daltons returned, the details of her underwear were known all over Fife. And pretty fancy stuff it is, too, I'm told. Not intended to keep her warm. Him, yes; her, no. Is that a better motive than a dead rabbit?'

'Yes,' Bruce said softly, 'I rather think it is.'

'Well, there was a lot more even than that.' Pelmann hesitated. 'I'm not going to tell tales about Fred Dalton. He's a friend. Ask him yourselves.'

'He was in Wormit,' I said. 'Or was he?'

Pelmann looked into our faces and was satisfied. He nodded and, without another word, settled himself in the Trooper and backed out into the road.

We had forgotten Hannah, standing silently by but listening intently. She was usually a respectful employee — far more so than Daffy — but something in Pelmann's revelations had touched a nerve. 'How you men stick together!' she said. 'He didn't want to snitch on a friend, but the friend's wife was another matter altogether. Men!'

'Don't be sexist,' I told her. Sometimes this nonsense about political correctness comes in useful.

Saturday had come round again. It was a week since Mrs Horner had died. To those who were not concerned about the manner of her going, the memory of her was already becoming something to be filed away and forgotten as quickly as possible. But among Alistair's friends and supporters, concern was growing and it was as if the woman's eternally inimical presence still brooded over us, awaiting the chance for more mischief.

Daffy was still absent and could be presumed to be enjoying the attentions of her husband. Our junior helpers had been carried off on various family ploys. Henry had decided that, if he had to drive to Kirkcaldy, he might just as well go the rest of the way, enjoy the fleshpots of Newton Lauder for an extra day and make an early start to whatever problems the young heiress had set him. He had driven off, first handing me a note from Mrs Hebden but refraining from making supposedly funny remarks about secret correspondence. Isobel had run out of her favourite homebrewed insecticide and confined herself in her little surgery while she mixed strange and dangerous potions. Bruce had eaten his usual late breakfast and was ready to leave for Mrs Horner's house, taking with him a sandwich for his lunch. I said that I'd have lunch at home and then, reluctantly, join him.

'Before you go,' I said, 'take a look at this.' I spread Mr Carmichael's photographs out on the kitchen table and singled out a shot of trees casting shadows over colourful dead bracken, against a background of the Moss. The only flaw in the composition was the presence of a car tucked away off the road and under one of the trees. 'These photographs were all taken on the morning Mrs Horner died. I know the place where this was taken. Walk out along Old Ford Road, bypass the sand-pit and follow the path and you come out here. I'm wondering why a car would be parked here, half hidden.'

Bruce peered at the scene. 'It might just have been left in the shade,' he suggested. 'You know how a car heats up on a day like that.'

'And,' I retorted, 'it might have been left by somebody who didn't want to be seen in the village and who therefore left it here and walked along by the burn below Old Ford Road to Mrs Horner's house. The registration number's legible. Isn't it worth a phone call to the DVLA at Swansea to find out?'

'I suppose so.'

I had no intention of wasting more time

and running up my phone bill. 'The call would come better from you, as a solicitor,' I said. 'You could make it from Mrs Horner's house.'

He agreed and hurried away, promising help at some unspecified time in the future.

Beth, Hannah and I were very short-handed for the morning's work, but with spasmodic assistance from Sam we managed to scramble through the cleaning and exercising and the morning feeds of the younger stock.

I had been awaiting my chance to get on with some serious dog-training, but first I had to deal with a minor rush of business. This brought a couple who thought that we ran an animal sanctuary and would be looking for a 'good home' for unwanted pups; and a young man who wanted a trained dog, couldn't afford it and settled for ordering a pup from our next litter.

He was followed by a former client in need of advice — free advice, I hardly need say. His spaniel seemed to be deficient in memory and a lesson learned one week would be forgotten by the next. Would I take the dog back for a crash course? I watched them work for a few minutes on the lawn and then explained gently that it would be a shame to take his money, which would be better spent if I were to take *him* for training. There was nothing wrong with the dog's memory. 'But,' I said, 'if dogs had two fingers, that's what he'd be giving you.' I told him again what I'd explained when he bought the dog, about the need to remain the leader of the pack, every minute of every day. He went away contrite and, he said, determined.

Before I could go and collect any of my trainees from the kennels, there was a ring at the doorbell. The others were busy, so I went to the door. I found a tall, sturdily built lady waiting impatiently. Her iron-grey hair was rigidly disciplined. She wore a linen suit in pale grey and 'sensible' shoes.

'About Mrs Horner's cat,' she said, without preamble.

I dislike talking business on the doorstep although sometimes there is no alternative. The table and chairs under the silver birch had been functioning almost as an outdoor office during the hot weather but the day had brought a cooler breeze off the North Sea. Moreover, something about the lady suggested that she would not fit comfortably into an informal setting. 'Come in,' I said. I led her into the sitting room and showed her a chair.

'You have the cat here?' she asked as soon as we were seated.

I find a terse and telegraphic mode of speech very infectious. 'Yes,' I said.

She blinked at me but went on. 'I was a friend of Jasmine Horner. I don't suppose that her nephew will take Hecuba on and I wouldn't want the old thing to be put down. I can offer her a good home.'

On the whole I rather approved of the suggestion. I hate to see an animal destroyed just because nobody has room or patience for it. But, little though I like the concept, animals are subject to ownership. This dislike may seem contradictory in one who regularly buys and sells them, but in my mind I can distinguish between my commercial activities and the dogs' subsequent existence as hunting partners. 'You'll have to speak to Mrs Horner's nephew,' I said. 'I wouldn't expect any difficulty, but it's not for me to say.'

Her expression led me to believe that she would sooner converse with any passing rapist. 'I would rather see the executor,' she said. 'I understand that he is living here. Is he available?'

Bruce would not welcome the interruption. Besides, I was sure that I knew the identity of this visitor and wanted to confirm my guess. She seemed to fulfil most of the criteria. 'I can have him phone you,' I suggested. 'I take it that you're Mrs Bullerton?'

She raised a formidable Roman nose and looked at me through eyes which, I noticed, seemed to be habitually slitted. 'Do I know you?' she asked.

'Not so far as I'm aware,' I said. 'But your name came up recently as having been a friend of Mrs Horner.' While I spoke, my mind had been working. I had seen Seagrove Cottages on the map. The former workmen's cottages, which I heard had been thrown together into a single more commodious residence, were at the further side of the Moss. They were approached from a byroad but there was a path across the far end of the Moss that led to the sand-pit and thence to Old Ford Road. 'And I think that you were seen walking towards your home and away from Mrs Horner's house at about the time that she died.'

Her nostrils flared. 'I hope that you're not suggesting — '

'I'm not suggesting anything,' I said. 'As far as I'm aware, you never quarrelled with her.'

'That's true. I certainly had no call to do her a mischief. Unlike yourself.'

I stared at her but there was no mischievous twinkle in her eye. Quite the reverse. 'Me?' I said. 'I argued with her about dogs once or twice. Apart from that, I hardly knew the woman.'

She frowned. 'Even after Jasmine Horner told the police that your bride had lied about her age?'

I shrugged. The matter had been so long ago that it was too late for anger. 'I never knew who was responsible for that piece of idiocy,' I said. 'In fact, the mistake was understandable. Beth always did look much less than her real age. When we married, Beth was twenty-four but she looked about fourteen. The local Bobby came up asking questions and Beth showed him her birth certificate and produced proof of her identity. That was more or less an end to it. In any case, I'd hardly have waited about ten years before taking revenge. Tell me, have the police taken a statement from you about your visit to Mrs Horner on the morning of her death?'

There was silence in the room. I waited. I was interested to see whether she would deny the visit, admit it, claim that she had already made a statement to the police or tell me to go to hell. Just when I was sure that an explosion was imminent, she suddenly sat back and relaxed. 'Why are you interested?' she asked.

'Some of us don't believe that Alistair Branch is guilty,' I told her.

'Nor do I,' she surprised me by saying. She had settled down for a cosy chat, apparently now accepting me as an equal. 'He seems a mild little man. I don't know what Jasmine had against him. But then, she had something against almost everybody. It was her absolute malevolence that kept me amused, and the fact that she could be relied on to dig up the dirt about practically anyone. But for that, I wouldn't have tolerated her for a minute. No, the police haven't spoken to me. I've been expecting a visit at any moment. If they don't come soon, I must go to them.'

'You know something that they don't?' I asked her.

'I don't know that I can offer them a better suspect than Alistair Branch,' she said, 'but yes. I do know something they don't.' She leaned forward and suddenly I recognized again the glint of malicious mischief that I had seen in Mr Pelmann and I knew what she and Mrs Horner had had in common. She was about to reveal a murky secret and she was loving it. 'I did visit Jasmine that morning,' she said. 'We had quite a chat. She was still very angry with her nephew for running away with Roland Bovis's wife. And that little *faux pas* had come on top of an earlier ruction about some silver that he'd sold for her. She had made up her mind at last. She was going to change her will.'

As far as I was aware that could only direct

suspicion in one direction. 'Mr Shute and Mrs Bovis were away sailing in the Adriatic,' I pointed out.

She shrugged that off immediately. 'There are such things as aeroplanes,' she said. 'And they don't even stamp your passport any more if you're coming from an EC country. Hire a car and walk the last mile or two. Child's play. He could have left the yacht and his mistress in some quiet harbour and have been back in two days. Who would know or care?'

'But he didn't know that she was going to change her will,' I said.

'There are also telephones,' she said impatiently. 'Think about it. He phones his aunt to ask if she's well and how the weather is at home and to tell her again that the lady's change of partners was by mutual agreement of the gentlemen involved. But his aunt is still angry. She says that she's going to change her will. The rest follows.'

What she was saying made a great deal of sense. What was more, it brought back into my mind the car in the photograph. I went to fetch it and put it into her hand. 'This was taken that morning. It must have been somewhere near your house,' I said.

'Just around the next corner.'

'Do you happen to know whose car that is?'

'It's certainly not mine. I had a central heating engineer at the house that day, but he came in a shabby old van.' She hesitated. 'His boss came along to check up on him,' she said reluctantly, 'and that could be his car. I just don't know.'

'That's very interesting,' I said slowly. 'You could be right. One person was seen, from a distance, who was almost certainly Mrs Horner's assailant. There's no suggestion that that person resembled Mr Shute, but I'm told that it could well have been Mrs Bovis.'

She shook her head impatiently. 'Emily Bovis was in the Adriatic on that Saturday.'

'You're sure?'

'Positive. She phoned me from Venice.'

'She could have *said* that she was in Venice?'

Again Mrs Bullerton gave an impatient shake of her head. 'When I got back from my visit to Jasmine, there was a message on my answering machine. I called her back. It was a Venice number.'

'But why did she call you?' I asked. I nearly added *of all people.*

'She is my daughter,' Mrs Bullerton said simply. 'So I know where she was. But her paramour is another matter. I asked Emily to call him to the phone. I wished to ask him once again to give up this ill-judged liaison.

But she said that he was out for a walk. If there is one place in the world not conducive to walking, unless one has the gift of walking on water, it is Venice. I suggest that my daughter was establishing her presence in Venice but that her lover was here, ensuring that his aunt did not have the chance to change her will.'

On consideration, I saw that it was possible. Not likely, but possible. 'Thank you,' I said. 'I'll make sure that the police have a word with you.'

'I'll look forward to that,' she said and I could see that she meant it.

* * *

Free at last, I sought out Isobel and found her, peering into her microscope, in the converted annexe which had become a small but efficient surgery. Before I could reopen a running argument as to whether Sid needed more steadiness training on dummies simulating rocketing pheasants, she looked round and asked me, 'Did the unfortunate Horace have fleas?'

'Strange question. I never saw him complete and alive,' I pointed out. 'The empty skin wasn't doing any scratching. Why?

'You said that Mrs Horner's cat was doing enough scratching for both of them. She's old and I'm told that she never went outside the garden. It looks like rabbit fleas again. Were there wild rabbits in the garden?'

'Not inside the wall. And little sign of rabbit damage. The walled garden looks pretty rabbit- and cat-proof, but of course gates have to be opened now and again. The police lab could determine whether Horace had fleas. Does it matter?'

Isobel shrugged. 'Not particularly. I thought you were collecting all the trivial pieces of evidence the police had missed. If Horace had passed fleas on to Mrs Horner's cat it would have been cast-iron evidence of something or other. Henry phoned, by the way. I thought you'd just left with Bruce, so he's going to phone you at Mrs Horner's house after he's seen the gun dealer. He said the gun's in beautiful nick and it's been proved for nitro powder.'

'In that case, I've got some money coming,' I said.

Isobel regarded me benignly. Sometimes she is like a sister to me, sometimes she takes on the role of a mother and just occasionally there are signs of something quite different. 'Well, don't go ploughing it all back into the business again this time.

182

Take Beth for a cruise or buy yourself something you really want.'

★   ★   ★

Sam, for once, lunched at home. He and I were first at the kitchen table. As we helped ourselves to sliced ham and salad I said, 'Sam, you know the Saturday that it happened to Mrs Horner? Last week?'

He nodded solemnly. He was slim rather than skinny but in other respects he looked so much like me that sometimes it took my breath away. 'The day we were asking questions about.'

'That's right. Do you happen to know what Mr Branch was wearing that morning?'

He munched thoughtfully before swallowing. 'No,' he said at last. 'But I'm going to see Audrey after lunch. She notices that sort of thing. I'll ask her.'

'I'll walk along with you,' I said. 'Or were you going to take your bike?'

'I'm walking. When I take my bike, Audrey rides it and then she falls off and blames me.'

'That's women for you,' I told him. 'Whatever goes wrong, it's always your fault. Be warned!'

We set off after lunch by my favourite path. It felt strange and unfamiliar to have my son

183

with me instead of one or more dogs. Sam prattled along the way. He had grown too big for his bicycle, he would like a Dundee United strip for Christmas and could he come beating the next time I went picking-up? I made vague but possibly affirmative replies, secure in the knowledge that he would soon have forgotten his more expensive desires or, if not, that I would be able to afford them out of my share of the Macnaughten shotgun. Again I could hear echoes of my own boyhood. Where had it gone, for God's sake? Where were the dreams now? I had been going to become prime minister, marry a film star, save the world. I gave myself a mental shake. I had had one career, I now had another which I loved and a family which I loved more. Did I really want to revert to the uncertainties, the agonies of youth? No, I decided. Middle age would suit me and damn the aches and pains.

Audrey's home was two houses short of the pub. She met us in the back garden. Her recollection of what everybody was wearing on the fatal Saturday was almost photographic although she could not remember seeing anyone wearing khaki shorts. I was left in little doubt that the first figure seen in the back lane by Mrs Guidman was Alistair and that those seen by her husband at the front of the houses could have been Mr and Mrs Jordan followed soon afterwards by Mr Dalton.

I left Sam with Audrey and bypassed the house to cross the road.

Bruce let me into Mrs Horner's house and I sat down with him for a discussion. 'No words from the Detective Superintendent,' Bruce said. 'Damn his eyes! Conscientious I may be but I don't make a habit of working at weekends. As I'm stuck here I may as well go on wading through this detritus.' He gestured at the partially sorted piles of paper split between the desk and any other flat surface. Receipts, letters, forms and photographs seemed to be mingled. 'Did I say that her filing system was modelled on the municipal tip?' Bruce asked me.

'You did. More than once!'

'I was unduly flattering, it isn't as orderly as that. I expect that she could put her hand on any scrap of paper at a moment's notice, but to the stranger it's a baffling confusion which all has to be sifted. You never know what may turn up in this sort of guddle.' Bruce frowned and bit his lip before deciding to go on. 'Between ourselves, I found a list of charities and a few words of draft which suggest that she may have been going to change her will and cut out Ian Shute, her

185

nephew. I gathered that she was furious when his partner's wife transferred her affections to the nephew.'

'As it happens, I can confirm that,' I said. 'The exchange seems to have been amicably managed between the parties, but Mrs Horner must have favoured the wronged husband.' I told him about Mrs Bullerton's revelations and her theory about the murder.

Bruce was nodding before I had finished. 'I've telephoned Swansea,' he said. 'That car belongs to Jacobsen's, the car-hire firm in Dundee. I've phoned their office but there's nobody there today outranking the girl who makes the tea and nobody's prepared to divulge the names of clients. So that particular line of enquiry will have to wait over.' He squinted at the papers in front of him. 'If I'm reading her simply awful writing correctly, which is a bit of a long shot, she intended to leave a legacy to Bovis as compensation.'

'Providing both men with motives?' I suggested.

'I wouldn't hang your hat on that,' Bruce said. 'Apart from both having alibis, which I presume have been checked for what they're worth, the legacy to Bovis would hardly have changed a pauper's lifestyle and what Mrs Horner had to leave wouldn't have made the nephew rich. She had almost nothing but the house itself, which isn't as big as it looks, the rooms are small and it needs a great deal of money spent on it. It doesn't even have central heating. So far as I can tell the old will stands. But I have to hunt for a holograph will or codicil, just in case she decided to do it herself, to the certain ultimate benefit of my profession. We make more revenue as a result of testators making their own wills than almost anything else.'

Except, I thought, *defending the clearly and indefensibly guilty*. I repeated Audrey's description of what Alistair had been wearing when Mrs Horner died but Bruce was unimpressed. 'A young girl may be a useful supporting witness but she's hardly 'best evidence',' he said. 'If you want to be helpful, you could go and ask Mrs Branch about clothes.'

A moment's thought satisfied me that even conversing with a weepy grass widow would be preferable to being dragooned into helping to inventory Mrs Horner's tawdry possessions. I went out again into the mild sunshine and walked past two houses. Who else, I wondered, was holding the keys of the absent McIntoshes? Had somebody hidden in the empty house, watching the comings and goings, emerging at the perfect moment to slay the dragon and frame St George . . . ? Somebody, perhaps, who was supposed to be sailing in the Adriatic, who had arrived and would depart by night? I shook my head at my own fevered imagination. I was finding it hard to picture any of these respectable, ordinary people picking up a waspish lady by the backside and shoving her head first into a water butt.

Alistair's sister-in-law was a small but determined lady who took me at first for a journalist or some other person trying to profit from her sister's trouble. She left me standing on the mat while she went to enquire about my *bona fides* and then led me through the house with a murmur of apology and left me with Mrs Branch.

Alistair's wife was bearing up better than I had expected. She was no longer the panic-stricken waif who had run all the way to Three Oaks. She had lost weight and her eyes were hollow, but she was in command of herself. I found her seated in the garden in the company of another lady, darning an obviously masculine sock as though absolutely confident that Alistair would be home, if not tomorrow then within a few days. I could only hope that her faith would not prove misplaced. June, Alistair's spaniel, lay unmoving at her feet, watching us with miserable eyes. I noticed that she was attached by a lead to the leg of a chair. Evidently, one lesson had been learned.

Mrs Branch's companion was a lady of around forty. Her hair was unashamedly grey, cut and styled with simple severity. She wore a plain cotton dress over her slightly full figure. Her face was round, friendly and still pretty in an innocent and virginal way. I was startled when Mrs Branch introduced her to me as Mrs Dalton. Her handshake was firm and absolutely platonic. I tried not to picture her in the exiguous underwear described by Mr Pelmann. The image came unbidden into my mind but failed to excite me.

There was a spare, flimsy garden chair beside her, evidently vacated by the sister-in-law, and I lowered myself carefully into it.

Answering my polite enquiry, Mrs Branch said that she was managing very well and her sister was a great comfort. People were being very kind. Any neighbour going to Cupar would offer her a lift so that she could visit Alistair or do some shopping. But there was word of Alistair being transferred to Perth, in which case things would become much more difficult until the police came to their senses.

'It won't be for long,' Mrs Dalton said in a softly musical voice, 'and you know that I'll drive you any time you like.'

Mrs Branch thanked her huskily. 'It was all spite, of course, on the part of that Detective Inspector,' she said. 'I've begun to remember, in bits. I seem to see him in uniform, which always makes it so difficult to recognize people when you meet them again in mufti. I think he was arguing with Alistair, and if I've got the right occasion it must have been the only time in his life that Alistair was made really angry. Not shouting angry but a cold rage. What it was about I don't remember, something to do with the car, I think. I'm sure the details will come back to me.'

'If they do,' I said, 'you must let Mr Hastie know. It could be useful. We're doing our best to find out the real facts.'

She put aside her darning and patted my hand. 'Bless you both!' she said. 'But do be as quick as you can. I can stick it out for however long it takes, but Iris can't stay for ever and June misses him terribly.' She looked down at the ageing spaniel. June had not even reacted to mention of her name. 'They're very close. I could almost believe that . . . But dogs don't die of broken hearts, do they?'

I had known several dogs who gave up the will to live when a beloved owner was taken from them, but it would have been cruel to say so.

'I've come to make an inquiry on behalf of

Bruce Hastie,' I said. 'He's tied up at the moment.'

As I spoke, thinking that Mrs Branch might prefer to keep our talk confidential, I glanced at Mrs Dalton. She flushed and jumped to her feet. 'I'll leave you to it,' she said. 'I wouldn't want to intrude.'

I could see that I had unintentionally hurt her feelings and hastened to try and put matters right. 'You're not bound to go — ' I began.

She turned away with a small gasp, but not before I had seen tears in her eyes. 'People are so cruel,' she said shakily and disappeared into the house.

Mrs Branch looked at me curiously. 'You do know about the way that Mrs Horner behaved towards her?' she asked.

I looked back at her blankly. 'I'm not on the main-stream for local gossip,' I said. 'Hardly anybody tells me anything, but I've just heard that the Daltons had a terrible row with her.'

Mrs Branch lowered her voice. 'You know about that? I'm not sure that I should be spreading gossip. It would lower me to her level.' But the strain in her face had lessened and the imp of mischief, rather than pure malice, was behind her eyes. I knew that she was dying to tell all.

'Any of the quarrels that she had with neighbours might be relevant', I said. 'Or at least they may show that plenty of people other than Alistair would cheerfully have drowned her in a water butt.'

'That's certainly true. I wouldn't have blamed Hector Dalton one little bit if he'd lost his temper with her.'

'Hector Dalton?' I said. 'Not his wife? I heard something about Mrs Horner snooping through their house and taking her friends with her.'

She picked up her darning again and seemed to be speaking directly to it. 'That was how it all started,' she said. 'Mrs Horner had the Daltons' key and she went through their house and let her friends go poking through the drawers and cupboards. And Beatrice Dalton may look very sweet and prim, and he may look quite . . . passionless, but people aren't always the way they look, are they?'

'Definitely not,' I said and, after a pause, 'Do go on.'

'Oh. Very well. Almost everybody for miles around heard all about it anyway. For a start, she dresses very modestly — never a trace of cleavage or a split skirt — but, from what we all heard, her underwear was from a very different shop. Artificial silk and frills and very, very provocative. Also, there was a long, blonde wig, so they said. And then — ' Mrs Branch paused and pursed her lips ' — it seems that Hector — such an unsuitable name — how shall I put it? — needed a little more help with his marital relations than just a little dressing up. Medical help. You know what I mean?' she finished.

'Viagra?'

'I'd guess that Viagra's too expensive for them. They know the value of money. Apparently it was something that he had to inject into himself. With a hypodermic needle. In the you-know-what. There!'

Mrs Branch picked up her darning again and set to work. Her face was pink but her expression was placid. Apparently she had found comfort in the recollection of somebody else's humiliation. I decided that if somebody had spread such a tale about me, true or not, I would definitely have resorted to violence.

I remembered what I had come for. 'Can you tell me what Alistair was wearing, that Saturday morning?'

'Oh yes,' she said. 'It was hot, wasn't it, that day? Alistair had white trousers left over from his cricketing days and a pale blazer, a sort of buff colour.'

'He never wears shorts?' I asked.

'No, never. He says that his knees are too knobbly.'

That seemed to cover the matter of Alistair's garb but there was one other question in my mind. 'What did I say that upset Mrs Dalton so much?' I asked.

Mrs Branch kept her head down over her darning but I was sure that I could detect barely suppressed amusement in her voice. 'After telling you so much I may as well tell you the rest. According to the rumours that circulated,' she said, 'there were several lengths of rope in their bedside locker along with the syringe and things.'

It took me a few seconds to get the implications. Then, 'Oh my God!' I said.

'You weren't to know. But just in case you feel like putting your foot in it again, perhaps I should tell you this. It all blew up again about ten days ago. As it happened, I was present, so I can vouch for what was said, if not for the truth of what was said. I was invited to tea by a lady in St Andrews. I don't know whether she did it on purpose, but she invited Mrs Horner and Beattie Dalton as well as several other ladies.

'Well, as you can imagine, it was very awkward. But Beattie couldn't leave without calling a taxi and it was soon obvious that she wasn't going to exchange a word with Mrs

Horner. In the end, after a lull in the conversation, Mrs Horner said loudly, 'Are you still not speaking to me?' Beattie kept her temper and just shook her head. And Mrs Horner said, 'Well, when you are, you'll have to tell me how your Hector looks in all those pretty things.'

'You can imagine the sort of silence that followed.

'That was the first suggestion there had ever been that Hector had . . . transvestite tendencies. And it may not have been true — how would Mrs Horner know? Beattie turned white but she kept her dignity. She just asked her way to the toilet and stayed there until her husband came to pick her up again. Nobody else said much but Mrs Horner chatted away about everything else under the sun, obviously as happy as Larry.'

I excused myself and departed as gracefully as I could. My face felt very hot and I was uncomfortably conscious of my hands and feet.

6

My shortest route would have been along the back lane but the back gate to Mrs Horner's house would still be bolted, so I returned by the way I had come. As I walked, I was wondering how on earth I could convince Mrs Dalton that I had been quite unaware of her bedroom secrets, without increasing her embarrassment by letting her know that I knew them now. Perhaps I could persuade Mrs Branch to tell her that I had spoken out of, and remained in, total ignorance. I tried, but failed, to think of something that I would have liked less than to have some such secret noised abroad. I was still flushed and probably muttering to myself.

Outside Mrs Horner's gate, a police Range Rover stood gleaming in the sunshine. I felt a twinge of apprehension. Fraser had kept his word. This would be make or break time. On the other hand I felt a simultaneous sense of relief that my mind would be distracted from my appalling *faux pas*. I knew only too well that from that day on I would often wake up in the small hours, hot and squirming with embarrassment, and, worse, it would be impossible to explain to Beth why I was so afflicted.

I approached with caution in case Inspector Blosson was waiting within, ready to pounce, but Sergeant Morrison was sitting at the wheel, alone in the vehicle, in uniform now but in shirtsleeve order. He looked hot and singularly fed up.

I came to his half-open window. 'Who's inside?' I asked.

'Detective Superintendent Fraser, DI Blosson and DS Parkes.' His likes and dislikes were clear from his tone. Towards the Detective Sergeant, he was neutral.

'When did they arrive?'

'Maybe ten minutes ago. The Super took a look around the garden. They've just gone inside, maybe a minute ago. Mr Blosson was looking ready to explode,' the Sergeant added with relish.

'Do they know about the rabbit yet?'

He shrugged. 'I wrote a report to DI Blosson, copied to Mr Fraser. If they've been into the office, they'll have seen it. Neither of them said anything.'

Bruce would certainly want my support. He might even now be phoning for me at Alistair's house, so my time was limited. 'Did you manage to get a copy of that photograph?' I asked softly.

He nodded. He looked at the house but a flowering hedge hid us at least from the ground floor windows. 'I shouldn't be doing this,' he said. 'I could be hung, drawn and quartered. But . . . ' He slid an envelope from his side pocket and passed it through the gap in the window. 'I'll want it back straight away.'

I extracted the photograph, which had been cropped from a larger print. It was sharp and had been taken at very close range. I studied it and returned it to the Sergeant. Not every man has been moved to pleasure by a photograph of a dog-turd in fine focus, but I was smiling inside as I handed back the envelope with a heartfelt word of thanks and went to the front door. Seeing it again, I noticed that the posts were both beginning to rot, down at the step. Serious maintenance was overdue.

The front door had been left off the latch, presumably for my benefit. I could hear voices from the sitting room so I knocked and looked in.

Fraser, now Detective Superintendent although I had last met him before he attained that lofty rank, was standing with his back to the fireplace in the attitude normally adopted by one who has every intention of staying in command of the proceedings. His ginger hair was thinning and becoming rather less gingery and he could now afford a better suit and a Carnoustie Golf Club tie, but otherwise he was as I remembered him. And it seemed that he remembered me and my foibles. 'Come in, *Mister* Cunningham,' he said. 'Mr Hastie was very anxious to have a word with me but he's been very reluctant to begin without your support.'

Bruce turned slightly pink. I was in no doubt that he resented the mild reproof. He was in sole occupation of the settee. 'Mr Cunningham made most of the discoveries that I want to bring to your attention,' he said stiffly. 'He can explain them and answer questions better than I can.'

'So you told me.' Fraser nodded to one of the easy chairs upholstered in synthetic leather and I seated myself.

'What's more,' I said, 'quite a lot of information has been handed to me since I last spoke with Mr Hastie.'

Detective Inspector Blosson was sitting very upright in the chair opposite, with an expression such as I had previously seen only on Isobel's face on an occasion when she had been examining the tail of a dog when the spaniel had suddenly passed wind in her face.

'I must protest,' Blosson said gruffly. 'With all due respect, this is not a proper investigation and it bears no resemblance to the official procedures.' In his perturbation, he was in great danger of tripping over his tongue.

Fraser looked towards the other man, presumably his sergeant, who was seated at the desk and taking what appeared to be competent shorthand. 'You may note the Inspector's protest,' he said, 'but Mr Cunningham has been helpful to us in the past and if he can help us to a better understanding of the facts I shall be grateful.'

Blosson's mouth tightened but he was not going to give up without a fight. 'Sir, I have made a thorough investigation and I have ascertained the facts,' he said. 'I have made an arrest. It only remains to complete the preparation of the case. I can do that without the interference of officious, bumbling amateurs. We're not living in a TV drama.'

There is seldom anything to be gained by making enemies. It must have been gall and wormwood to the Detective Inspector to have his superior picking over his recent work in front of laymen and I had been wondering how to speak out while saving his face, but that consideration suddenly went by the board. After being referred to as a bumbling amateur, I was quite prepared to see the Detective Inspector's face in close contact with the dog-poo which had contributed to the arrest of Alistair Branch. I was careful in choosing words which would certainly sting. 'I'm sure that Detective Inspector Blosson has carried out the investigation to the utmost of his ability,' I said gently. 'I can only tell you that I have been making very little effort in that direction. Most of the information I have picked up came to me simply because I listened to anyone who wanted to speak to me and thought about what they told me. Their information was all available to the investigating officers. Following it up, I took a cursory look around with the help of a . . . friend. That's all. And yet I have come up with indications that what little evidence exists against Alistair Branch was fabricated and I have found several other people with just as much opportunity and stronger motives.'

'Motives don't make cases,' Fraser said warningly.

'Obtaining hard evidence is your business, not mine. Even so, I have some. And if, as I can show, the evidence against Alistair Branch was tampered with, you have nothing against him but the motive of a quarrel over a dog-turd. How do you fancy bringing that up in court?'

'If you have been tampering with evidence,'

Blosson said in a shaking voice, 'or influencing witnesses, I'm going to *have* you, my lad.'

That did it. 'I also learned,' I said, 'that there had been trouble between this person, your Detective Inspector, and Mr Branch in the past. I believe this arrest to have been motivated by spite following on from some past grievance.'

There was a moment of horrified silence. I saw Bruce flinch and I hoped to God that Mrs Branch had not been wool-gathering. I had put my head on the block and Alistair's beside it.

Blosson's face had gone from white to scarlet and back to white again. He hesitated over the choice between a dozen explosive replies and as a result for a moment he merely gibbered. Fraser looked at him thoughtfully and got in first. 'Is this true?' he asked.

'Certainly not,' Blosson snapped. 'I resent this accusation and, if you'll leave it to me, sir, I will take appropriate action.'

'I'm sure that you would. Have you ever encountered Mr Branch in the past?'

'I have no recollection of doing so. None at all.'

Fraser studied him for several seconds and then turned his attention to me. 'I hope that you're wrong,' he said, 'but for your sake I have to hope that you have some reason, good or not, for what you've said.'

'I understand that it happened while Mr Blosson was still in uniform and that it may have had to do with a traffic incident,' I said. My mouth had gone dry.

'Then it should still be on record,' Fraser said. 'Sergeant, get on to Records and see if they can trace any such event.'

'The phone's in the hall,' Bruce said. It was the first time that he had opened his mouth since passing the buck to me (whatever, I thought in a moment of escapist frivolity, a buck might be in the context.)

The Sergeant was a tall man who had to be near the age for retirement. His face was totally impassive. He got up without a word and left the room.

Blosson began to speak but Fraser held up a hand. 'We'll wait,' he said. I had always known him for a fair man. He was not going to come down on either side until the facts were in the open. Blosson subsided but he was a burning fuse.

In the silence that followed, I could hear the Sergeant's voice in the hall. But I had to get my knowledge into the open quickly, while I still had their ear and a degree of trust from Fraser. 'While we're waiting,' I said, 'do you have a photograph of the evidential dog faeces available?'

Fraser looked at Blosson again. The Detective Inspector hesitated and then, with a show of reluctance, lifted a briefcase from beside his chair. After a brief hunt he produced a larger print of the photograph I had already seen, handing it to the Detective Superintendent. 'It's nothing more or less than a piece of shit,' he said to me, 'the same as you're talking.'

'That,' said Fraser, 'is more than enough of that.'

Sergeant Parkes returned almost immediately. 'They'll call us back,' he said.

'In the meantime,' Fraser said, 'we may as well hear what Mr Cunningham has to say about the evidence.'

He handed me the photograph. In this enlargement the turd was now several times life-size and the image was still razor-sharp. I made a pretence of studying it, for Sergeant Morrison's sake. 'There's no doubt about it,' I said. 'If this had been deposited in the gateway of this house, one might expect, perhaps, to see the surface dusted with road grit and possibly sand left over from last winter's snow clearance. Instead, if you look closely, you can see what look like grass seeds embedded in it and several small grass stems.

There's even a portion of grass blade. And I think that you'll find that the black specks are rape seed. When your forensic scientists examine it, they'll have to agree that this was transferred from the lane behind the houses, which is where Mr Branch said all along that he walked.'

'Let me see that.' Blosson got up and snatched the photograph out of my hand. He carried it to the window and studied it for a full minute before coming back to stand over me. He glared at me, but I had the impression that he was looking between my eyes rather than into them. 'You interfered with this specimen before we uplifted it,' he said at last.

I leaned back to escape the smell of his sweat. 'You can see for yourselves,' I said, 'that that suggestion is ridiculous. If I had known of its existence, which I did not, and had I wished to tamper with it, which I wouldn't, I would only have had to take a stick and flick the evidence across the road and into the rough ground beyond, where it would have been lost for ever or have become meaningless. Can you really picture me sprinkling it with grass seed, just to invalidate it as evidence?'

Fraser looked at the Detective Inspector with raised eyebrows.

'I did not move it, I swear to God,' Blosson said in a shaking voice.

'I never thought that you did,' Fraser said, but I could see that Blosson's outburst had put the thought into his mind. He held out his hand for the photograph.

Blosson, returning to his chair, paused to put it into his hand.

'And I never suggested it,' I said, 'although I'm amazed that a DNA test was obtained without the lab being asked for any more detailed comment.' I was tempted to suggest that mention might have been made of the grass and seeds and might have been suppressed, but I was afraid of alienating Fraser as well as Blosson. Fraser was capable of seeing the point for himself. 'I'm only suggesting that without the evidence of the dog-turd and the cigar butt, both of which could have been transferred from the back lane, you have only a weak motive to offer against Mr Branch and there were several others with more pressing ones.'

'In fact,' said Bruce, 'I suggest that you have no justification for holding my client any longer and that you may as well release him immediately on police bail while awaiting the result of a more thorough investigation.'

'A more *competent* investigation,' I said.

Blosson leaned forward, prepared to erupt

but Fraser frowned him into stillness and silence. Fraser, I decided, had learned the habit of command since we had last met. 'A little while longer won't do Mr Branch any great harm,' he said. 'We'll see how quickly the lab can report on those seeds and what they say about them. And, of course, what else Mr Cunningham has to tell us.'

I took a few seconds to arrange my thoughts in tidy sequence. Blosson's malevolent glare distracted me. I looked up at the ceiling. 'The physical evidence,' I said, 'has to be seen along with the testimony of Mrs Guidman, who was at her kitchen window all morning and looking across the corner of the field towards the back lane. She was keeping an eye on the movement of pigeon over the rape field on her husband's behalf. She's pretty certain that she saw Mr Branch go home by that way and her description of the person's clothing and of his dog both tally. Very shortly afterwards, she saw a different figure emerge from the back gate of this house, do something surreptitious which involved some stooping and go back in through the gate.'

'I tried to interview her,' Blosson said. His posture had begun to alter subtly. As the flaws in his investigation emerged, he seemed less like a tiger narrowly restrained from attacking its prey and more like the prey, defiant but running out of time. He ran a finger round his collar. I could see sweat on his upper lip. 'There was never anybody at home when I called.'

In for a penny, in for a pound . . . 'Or else your reputation had gone before you and she was afraid to answer the door,' I said.

Blosson was roused from defensiveness to renewed indignation. 'Are you calling me a bully?'

'You have that reputation. If the cap fits . . . I suggest that the person Mrs Guidman saw was collecting this excrement and a discarded cigar butt.'

'I suggest that that's no more than a wild guess,' Blosson said furiously.

'And I suggest,' Bruce said, 'that on the present evidence you clearly cannot justify holding my client any longer. That is all that we're here for.'

'Not so fast,' Blosson said. 'There's more evidence. You don't know the result of the post mortem yet.' He looked enquiringly at his superior.

'Go on,' Fraser said. He was concentrating intently but giving no sign of which way his thoughts were going.

Blosson groped in his briefcase again and came out with a typed and stapled document.

He leafed through it and licked his dry lips. 'There had been no time for bruises to develop but the pathologist found marks on either side of the deceased's hips, consistent with a pair of hands taking a grip. He also found a small bloodstain, Group O — which is Mr Branch's group — on her skirt in a position corresponding to the fingers of the right hand of her assailant. Mr Branch had a recent small cut on his third finger.'

'At any given moment,' I said, 'about one man in three has a recent scar on a hand.' I held up my right hand. A barbed-wire scratch was still livid on my palm. 'Especially those of us who live in the country and do our own gardening. Tell me, were there any other marks on the body?'

Blosson was on the point of inviting me to go to hell but Fraser spoke first. 'Tell us,' he said.

Blosson pursed his lips but began to leaf through the report. 'You'll not be wanting her state of health and old appendix scars,' he said. 'There's only . . . Here it is. 'A puncture wound about four days old on the left thigh, made with a blunt but pointed instrument such as a belt buckle.' Look for yourself if you like.' He held out the document.

'I'm satisfied,' I told him.

'What was Mrs Horner's blood group?' Bruce asked.

Blosson hesitated. 'Also Group O,' Fraser said. Blosson's mouth snapped shut. I heard his teeth click.

'I understand,' said Bruce, 'that the deceased's left earring had been torn from her ear. If her attacker pulled it loose, he might easily have got blood on his fingers. He may then be assumed to have dropped the earring, apparently by accident, into the butt and when Mrs Horner looked or reached down into the water he lifted her by the hips and pushed her in, transferring her own blood to her skirt in the process. Or if the earring was pulled off accidentally by a twig, he might have got blood on his fingers from the earring in picking it up and, again apparently by accident, dropping it into the water butt.'

Blosson started to protest but again Fraser signalled for him to wait. 'Mr Hastie is correct,' he said. 'I have to decide first whether we have enough of a case to justify holding a respectable man in custody — always a serious matter for him and one not to be treated lightly. I think that we should meet this Mrs Guidman straight away. Sergeant, would you telephone and ask her if we can pay her a visit or, if she prefers, she would come to us here?'

'I don't think that she trusts telephones,' I said. 'She equates them with computers and smart bombs.'

'In that case, Sergeant, go and convey the invitation.'

The Sergeant got up again. 'Very good, sir. Where do I go?'

'If you go out of the back gate,' I said, 'and look to your right, you'll see that the lane goes through to the village street between the corner house — Mr Bovis's — and the smaller house to the left as you look at them, which is where the Guidmans live.'

The Sergeant gave me a nod of thanks and left the room. We heard his footsteps crunch over the gravel.

Fraser looked from me to Blosson. His glance was speculative, as if at specimens in a bottle. He was weighing us up and when he had made up his mind he would come down hard on one of us, but I took comfort from the fact that, whatever the outcome for Alistair, already the evidence of a sloppy investigation was piling up. 'I think,' he said to me, 'that we can manage without the *chiel amang us takin' notes* while you give me an outline of just what other evidence you have uncovered.'

'Are you aware that she was a vicious and

spiteful woman who made a hobby out of courting unpopularity?' I asked him.

'No,' Fraser said, frowning, 'I wasn't told that.'

'A gross exaggeration,' Blosson said. 'Gross.'

'A word with any of the locals would confirm what I have just said,' I retorted. 'Even her close friend Mrs Bullerton said much the same only today. I've met the type before, in the army. It usually stems from one or the other of two attitudes — high or low self-esteem. The swollen-headed may think, 'They're all stupid, how dare they judge me?' And somebody else with a profound inferiority complex may recover some confidence from being a focus of attention, a thorn in the public flesh, and getting away with it.'

'To which group would you suggest Mrs Horner belonged?' Fraser asked curiously.

I remembered a corporal who had plagued a year of my army service and an unsatisfactory kennel-maid whom we had got rid of as fast as the legislation would allow. 'There's a middle group,' I said. 'Non-achievers who think that the world owes them a better deal. They can have both attitudes at the same time.

'As one example of her malevolence, you've

212

had a report on the find we made in the garden?'

'I glanced at Sergeant Morrison's report,' said Fraser. 'I had difficulty seeing it in any sensible context.'

'No wonder,' Blosson said. 'It's a load of rubbish!'

'Have you had a lab report on the rabbit skin?' I asked.

'I ran the evidence over to the lab straight away,' Blosson said, 'just to see what sort of stunt you were trying to get away with. But it's rabbit skin all right.' He took a few stapled pages out of his case and almost threw them at Bruce, who passed them more gently to me. I scanned quickly through the scientific officialese.

'Spell it out for me,' Fraser said.

I took him through the tale of the luckless Horace from the first inkling picked up by an anonymous source, through the hunt by Jason in Mrs Horner's garden to the excavation of the remains. It was clear that neither of them had taken in the full implications of Sergeant Morrison's report. If Blosson looked surprised, Fraser seemed to be hiding genuine disgust. I had thought that a senior policeman would have seen it all before, but apparently a neighbour who would kill and eat a little girl's pet rabbit was more abhorrent to him than the average criminal. 'If that was typical of her behaviour,' he said, 'we need have no shortage of suspects. Are you suggesting Mr or Mrs Pelmann for the role?'

Bruce was nodding but I shook my head. 'That's for you to weigh up,' I said. 'But probably not. For one thing, neither of them bears any resemblance to Mrs Guidman's description of the figure that came out of the gate. For another, somebody told the Pelmanns that the information had reached the police from me and Mr Hastie here. Pelmann came to see us. He was indignant and his manner was threatening, but it didn't suggest guilt to me.'

Detective Superintendent Fraser glanced again at the Detective Inspector. 'I let it slip,' Blosson said. 'Accidentally.'

'We'll discuss it later,' Fraser said. 'Who else?'

'It would be quicker to list the people who *didn't* owe her a grudge,' I said. 'How about Mr and Mrs Dalton from further along the road? When they were innocent newcomers, they left their key with Mrs Horner while they went abroad. She gave her few friends a conducted tour and the Daltons' most intimate secrets were causing hilarity all over the neighbourhood in no time flat. Ten days ago, I'm told, Mrs Horner went further and made, in company, a totally unforgivable suggestion arising from the same invasion of the Daltons' privacy.'

'What intimate secrets?' Fraser asked.

'I don't think that it's for me to tell you. But,' I said grimly, 'if anybody, male or female, ever treated me that way, there would certainly be violence done and to hell with the consequences.' Truth to tell, I was still a little sensitive about my brick-dropping. Perhaps the Daltons would take their revenge by spreading the tale of my clumsiness around. 'A few tactful questions would be all that was needed. But take note of this. A lorry came by from the direction of the sand-pit at almost exactly the moment that the Pelmanns heard Mrs Horner cry out. If you accept that that was when she went into the water butt, Mr Guidman, who was on the Moss, saw Mr Dalton walking towards this house and the village very shortly afterwards. I'm told that Mrs Dalton joined her husband for lunch at the hotel. That doesn't prove anything. I suppose that Mrs Dalton could have done the deed and hurried on to join him. But she looks quite unlike the figure that Mrs Guidman describes.'

'There are more?' Fraser asked.

'Certainly there are more,' I said. It seemed

a good moment to throw names at him. 'Who would you like next? Mrs Bullerton herself admits that she visited here that morning but the lorry driver saw her walking away from the village towards her home.'

'Well, then — ' Fraser began.

'But,' I said — Fraser groaned — 'her daughter is married to Mr Bovis next door to here. She has left him for her husband's partner, who is Mrs Horner's nephew. Bovis is the type of charming rogue that many women dote on. A very suitable person to be out and about buying antiques at the door, although I suppose that a wife could soon tire of being married to a charming rogue. Mrs Horner seems to have favoured Bovis against her nephew during an earlier row about the value of a pair of silver candlesticks; and then she was furious with her nephew for leading Mrs Bovis, as she would regard it, astray.

'This is where you may feel that it gets interesting. Mrs Horner therefore intended to cut the nephew out of her will. Mr Hastie found notes to that effect and Mrs Bullerton states that Mrs Horner told her of that intention.'

'Another motive,' Fraser said.

'True,' I said. 'Ian Shute, Mrs Horner's nephew and beneficiary, is a partner in the antique shop. The shop shows all the signs of a serious cash flow problem. The assistant tells me that they suffered a serious loss by buying a major item which turned out to have been stolen. I can't think of any profession more dependent on the availability of capital than the world of antiques.'

'Perhaps I shouldn't say this,' Bruce put in, 'but as motives go it's not a very strong one. Mrs Horner had little to leave and this house is small and run down. And — this is in confidence for the moment — she had raised a mortgage on it. If there's any life assurance, I haven't found a trace of it. Not a valuable legacy at all.'

'Moreover,' I said, 'Mrs Bullerton is also adamant that her daughter really was in Venice that day and that she spoke to her there on the phone. Whether or not she would lie for her daughter is for you to decide.

'The assistant in the shop, Mrs Judith Tolliver, told me that Ian Shute was also on the phone from Venice that morning. I don't know whether she could have told the difference if he had phoned from here and told her that he was calling from Venice, but the Telecom records might tell you. And, of course, I don't know whether Mrs Tolliver would lie for him. For all I know, they're lovers.'

'That's not for you to worry about. As you implied, investigation is our business.' As he spoke, Fraser was watching Blosson out of the corner of his eye. 'All these aspects must be checked out, and thoroughly. Go on. Who else?'

'There's Mrs Bullerton herself,' I said. 'She seems to have been walking away from the scene around the time that we think Mrs Horner was killed. But she could have reversed her steps when she heard the lorry coming. And how certain can we be of the time? Could the voice have belonged to somebody other than Mrs Horner?'

'It's a possibility,' Fraser said.

'The question was rhetorical,' I said, 'because, from what Mrs Guidman will tell you, I think that the murderer was probably a man. But not necessarily. The figure she saw was described to me as thickset and dark-haired. I don't know Mrs Bovis by sight, but a busty woman can look thickset.'

'Even at a distance,' Fraser said, 'the legs would give her away, surely.'

'The legs would be hidden by the crop. Oilseed rape grows almost to waist height.'

Blosson jerked upright. 'Then how do you suppose this Mrs — what is it? — Guidman saw the dog?'

He had a valid point and it gave me a jolt.

Perhaps I had been coasting along too easily. 'You'll have to ask her that,' I said. 'I've never seen the view from her window.

'Another point, if the killing was not premeditated, the murderer was almost certainly a man — a very local man, to have observed where Mr Branch threw his cigar end and where his dog decided to squat. It would spoil his plan to leave clues to somebody who was elsewhere that day. Very few women would have had a small cigar handy, ready to drop ash onto the dead woman's back and add to the incrimination of Alistair Branch. I'm told that Mr Jordan was handing out small cigars to celebrate the birth of a granddaughter, but he would be unlikely to force them on the womenfolk.'

'For all the ash that would have been needed,' Fraser said, 'anybody could have picked up another cigar butt. After the long drought, you could expect there to be a number lying where Mr Branch habitually walked. Not that I necessarily go along with the theory, I'm just making the point.'

'Point taken,' I said. 'Mrs Horner's nephew is supposed to have been sailing in the Adriatic with Mrs Bovis. When Mrs Bullerton asked to speak to him, her daughter said that he had gone for a walk. Whether or not he made a secret return visit here is a matter for you to check. If he got wind of the impending change to his aunt's will — and, remember, he may not have known how short of money she was — he could have flown back to Britain, arrived here in darkness, hidden — perhaps in the empty house next door — and emerged to do the deed. There was a hired car parked near Seagrove Cottages, where Mrs Bullerton lives, on the Saturday. Allan Carmichael can provide you with a photograph.'

'Well,' Fraser said, 'you've certainly suggested a few — '

'I haven't quite finished,' I said.

Fraser sighed. 'There's *more*? Go on, then.'

'I have been getting hints,' I said, 'that Mrs Horner had laid a complaint with the police about a dog having bitten her and that a summons had been issued. I understand that the incident was recent. You'll notice that the pathologist mentioned a puncture wound without referring to it as a bite. I would suggest that she made the mark herself and showed it to her doctor. I presume that the death of the only witness will result in the summons being withdrawn.'

Fraser looked at Blosson. 'Do we know of such a summons?' he asked sharply.

Blosson hesitated but he must have reasoned that whatever enquiries he had made leading to his knowledge of the summons would be on record. 'Mr Jordan,' he said. 'The end house.'

'I hardly know the Jordans,' I said. 'I'm not sure that I'd recognize them if we met in the street. But I do know their dog. They leave him to board with us whenever they go away. A miniature apricot poodle called, for some reason, Hamlet. He's a very charming little dog and loves people. His usual greeting is to butt you in the back of the leg. Mrs Horner, with her almost pathological hatred of dogs, might well have mistaken it for an attack and added an apparent tooth-mark to strengthen the case and increase the likelihood of a destruction order on the dog.'

'But Mr Jordan's a councillor,' Fraser said. 'He's on the Police Board.'

'I haven't accused him of anything more than having a very strong motive,' I said. If Fraser thought that being a councillor guaranteed honesty, he was more innocent than the officer I remembered.

7

Fraser was about to say more, no doubt to press me for more information although my store of fact and speculation was exhausted. To my relief the Sergeant returned, leading Mrs Guidman gently by the hand.

We stood up. I had never met Bob's wife. She turned out to be a small woman — I tend to be as thin as a thumb-stick but I would have made at least two of her. Her face, under a crown of silvery hair, had the same innocence as Mrs Dalton's. It was lined but the bone structure had a certain purity and it was a kindly face, the face of one whom I could imagine doing small obligements for her neighbours, if she could put herself forward enough to face them. There was no doubt that she was either very shy or very timid. She clung to the Sergeant's hand for reassurance until he had led her to a chair and persuaded her to sit down.

'I don't think that I need detain you gentlemen during this,' Fraser told Bruce and me.

'We'll go and get on with something more constructive,' Bruce said.

Mrs Guidman looked terrified at the prospect of being left alone with three policemen. 'Just tell the man what you told Bob to tell me,' I said soothingly. It occurred to me that I might be able to divert a little of Blosson's aggression. 'By the way,' I said, 'how did you manage to see Mr Branch's dog, with the rape standing so high?'

'He jamp up on the troch,' she replied.

That seemed to close the subject before it had opened. 'Mr Fraser will look after you,' I said.

She nodded but I still hesitated. I had no grounds for insisting that I remained present while the police interviewed a witness, but I was sure that Blosson's hostility, which was hovering in the room like a swarm of killer bees, would reduce anyone as timid as Mrs Guidman to jelly.

Detective Superintendent Fraser either took the hint or sensed my disquiet, or perhaps he had a similar concern of his own. 'Mr Blosson,' he said. 'Take the Range Rover and go back to the office. Complete your report up to date. I shall want to see it on my desk first thing on Monday morning.'

Blosson got to his feet and stood to attention. 'Mr Fraser,' he said, 'I think that I have a right to be present. My competence and impartiality have been called into question.'

'You will be kept fully informed and will have the opportunity to answer any allegations,' Fraser said tonelessly. 'Leave Sergeant Morrison on guard here and send somebody back with the car.'

It seemed to be a good moment to escape.

★   ★   ★

Bruce crossed the hall to the dining room but I hurried quickly up to the half-landing where a window gave me a partial view of the back lane over the garden wall. And there, about opposite Alistair Branch's house, was the cattle trough — a former bath, as was quite customary among thrifty Scots farmers. The farmer had even fitted it with a lid to prevent it filling with water and algae while the field was in crop and not being used as pasture. Detective Inspector Blosson would not so easily pick holes in Mrs Guidman's account.

I joined Bruce in the dining room.

'I think you've cracked it,' Bruce said. 'They'll have to let Alistair go after this.' He was still hugging his clipboard. 'Blast!' he snorted. 'I've left all my other papers in there. Do you think I could go back?'

'No way!' I said. 'Fraser's coaxing out of

Mrs Guidman the very information you've been looking for. He'll be trying to create the right atmosphere of confidence and trust. She saw Alistair going home by the back way and she saw the murderer. Fraser's doing your job for you. That particular boat is not one for rocking. For God's sake put your feet up and relax for a minute or two.'

Bruce walked round in a small circle on the worn dining-room carpet, frowning into space. 'If I sit still at a time like this,' he said fretfully, 'I'll get anxiety symptoms. I *must* learn to avoid getting steamed up over a client's affairs. The trouble is, I like Mr Branch.' He sighed deeply. 'The one thing that always relaxes me is to put another task behind me. Well, there's only one other useful thing I can do without the rest of my papers. We'll just have to get on with the inventory. You call it out to me and I'll write it down.'

I was hardly in a position to plead another engagement. I had shot my bolt. I could have left him and gone home but my curiosity was now fully engaged. 'All right,' I said. 'Until they come out of there. Where do you want to begin?'

'Do you know anything about furniture?'

I know a little about antique furniture but listing Mrs Horner's tawdry bits and pieces was not my idea of fun. 'I can tell a table from a chair,' I said.

Bruce sighed again, even more deeply. 'Then let's start with the pictures,' he said. 'Just call out the dimensions, a rough description and the name of the artist if you can read it.'

He handed me a small retracting measuring tape. Fired by a little of Henry's enthusiasm at second hand, I have learned a little about pictures but I was not impressed by the examples adorning Mrs Horner's walls. The room had been heated by coal fires for generations. The paintings, which had to be family heirlooms, were dark with old varnish and the soot of ages. I read off the dimensions of the first painting. 'Oil painting. Signature could be Amos or Ames. Possibly Anus. Highland Cattle sinking slowly into a bog. The frame's a fake, papier mâché painted gold.' I turned the frame round but there was no label on the back.

'Next. Watercolour, very faded, slightly fly-spotted. Signature totally illegible but Russell Flint it is not. Snow scene with rocks and a stag. Thin oak frame. No label. Next. Oil. A loch, looks like Loch Linnhe, from what I can see under the yellow varnish. I can't see a signature but there's a label on the back. Horatio McCulloch, whoever he may have been. Good Victorian frame, wood gilt. Next. Oil again. Portrait of a Victorian paterfamilias with a distinct squint. Facial resemblance to a frog, if accurate, suggests that he may have been an ancestor of Mrs Horner. Signature J. Burdock. Frame probably worth more than the portrait. Last one. Flowers, executed in tapestry, very faded. That's the lot in here.'

Bruce frowned at his clipboard. 'Not very definitive, is it? Hardly enough to get a valuation on. We don't even know enough to tell whether any of them would justify the expense of getting them cleaned. For all we can tell, one of them could be painted over a Rembrandt. I'd better get an expert in.'

'Roland Bovis lives next door,' I told him. 'You know who I mean? He's in partnership with Mrs Horner's nephew in that antique shop in Broughty Ferry. He's often away at the sales on a Saturday but he might be at home. At least if he makes a fee from it the money stays in the firm. Shall I phone him?'

Bruce considered. 'I can't see any objection,' he said. 'It would only be preliminary, to get the descriptions right and tell me whether anything here should be restored or sent to auction. He has a connection with the sole beneficiary, so any significant figures would have to be submitted to an independent valuer, but you don't have to tell him that.'

There was a directory under the hall table. I dialled Bovis's number. He answered after five or six rings and recognized my voice. 'I'm speaking from next door,' I said, 'assisting the executor. Would you care to give us some help with the inventory and valuation?'

There was a pause. 'If it doesn't take too long,' he said. 'I'll come round now.'

Bruce joined me in the hall. By the time that we had measured and listed a poor Victorian painting of a puppy and kittens by somebody signing himself or herself W. Ratling, Bovis was at the door and the telephone was ringing. I introduced Bruce to Bovis and let them get on with it.

DS Parkes had come out to answer the telephone on the assumption that it would be his call back from Records but, 'It's for you,' he said, passing me the phone.

Henry was on the line. 'I've shown Keith the gun,' he said. 'It's still in proof and in excellent condition. He says he'll give you eight hundred for it, or you might get more if he sells it for you on commission.'

'Hang on,' I said. 'Bovis is here now. I'll ask him.'

I followed Roland Bovis into the dining

228

room and put the question to him for a decision. He said, 'We'll take the eight hundred. Definite profit today's usually worth at least as much as possible profit tomorrow.'

I went back to the phone. 'Grab the money and run,' I told Henry.

'That's what I thought he'd say. If he's near by, make sure that he can't hear me.'

Bovis was still in the dining room with Bruce and the door was shut. 'He can't,' I said.

'According to the auctioneer, Shute and Bovis don't get to purchase on credit any more. It's cash up front or no deal. And I forget what you said he said he paid for it, but he only paid sixty-five. A rip-off merchant! By the way, did Bovis say that he came to the auction last week?'

I felt the hairs stir on the nape of my neck. But it is never easy to recall the exact words of an earlier conversation. 'That's what I understood him to mean,' I said cautiously.

'Well, he didn't, again according to the auctioneer. He went there the day before and left bids on anything he fancied or where he thought the reserve was set too low.'

'That could be interesting.' The sudden realization that the apparently perfect alibi of a neighbour was flawed gave a stir to the nebulous thoughts brewing in my mind and one half-digested item floated to the surface. The door to the dining room was still closed. 'Henry,' I said, 'you're the picture fancier around here. The name Horatio McCulloch sounded made up but the more I think about it the more I think that I hear bells ringing.'

'I should think that you *would* have heard it before.' There was more animation in Henry's voice than I had heard for a long time. 'One of his paintings — Kilchurn Castle on Loch Awe — was sold by Sotheby's in an auction at Gleneagles recently. It made more than a quarter of a million. So it was just as well that I didn't fancy it one damn bit.'

★　★　★

Back in the dining room, Bovis was speaking to Bruce. ' — told me that her father bought this house in the twenties. He was a younger son and although he had a few family bits and pieces he was pinched for cash and most of the furniture would have been considered cheap and nasty even at the time.'

'And the pictures?' I broke in. 'What sort of figure would you put on this one?' As if by chance, I pointed to the Horatio McCulloch.

He managed not to jump but I saw a muscle twitch in his cheek and I thought that his eyes changed focus. He knew, all right. He had probably done Mrs Horner's insurance valuation for her. 'One fifty on a good day,' he said.

I knew then what I should have seen before. It came to me with absolute certainty and I was saddened. Roland Bovis had seemed a likeable rogue, a type to which I sometimes feel drawn if only because their approach to life is the very opposite of mine. I preferred to be solid and responsible but there were times when I wished that I had the temperament, as Daffy once phrased it, to 'throw my knickers over the windmill.' But Bovis had gone much, much too far. I glanced down at his legs. He was wearing shorts and his legs were white.

I closed the dining-room door behind me, knocked and put my head into the sitting room. Mrs Guidman was sitting composedly beside the fireplace. Sergeant Parkes at the desk had paused in his shorthand. The absence of Detective Inspector Blosson gave the gloomy room almost a festive air.

Fraser looked round. 'A word with you,' I said. 'I think it's urgent.'

Rather than put Mrs Guidman out into the hall he came out and joined me, half closing the door behind him. 'Bovis is your man,' I told him. 'Definitely.'

'Bovis?'

231

'Sh! He's here now.' I indicated the dining-room door. 'He's the man who Mrs Guidman saw.'

Fraser's eyebrows went up. He took my sleeve and drew me silently into the sitting room. 'Could Mr Bovis have been the man you saw come out of the back gate?' he asked Mrs Guidman.

'Aye,' she said quietly. 'I thocht it was him at the time.'

'Go on about him,' Fraser said to me. We were still standing just inside the sitting-room door, too rapt to sit down.

'A lorry driver from the sand-pit saw somebody of his description and wearing shorts such as he has on at the moment, standing on the other side of the road and looking down towards the Moss. I thought that it might have been the killer, newly arrived by the path down by the burn and turned away to hide his face from the lorry driver. But now I think that Bovis was on the way round to pay one of his calls on Mrs Horner and waiting for his dog to come back from doing its business among the bushes. They'd have come out of his side gate and in at her front gate and nobody need have seen them. He has a dog which hates all cats and she had a cat which hates all dogs, but against all the odds the two animals, it seems, got on

232

well together — like must have been calling to like. He's the one dog that Mrs Horner was prepared to tolerate. When Bovis came to see me, the day after the murder, the dog had fleas.'

Fraser was looking slightly stunned. 'Is all this relevant?' he asked. 'We seem to be wandering a long way from the point.' I was surprised that he expressed himself so mildly. It was a confused tale but I was trying to pack a maximum of information into a minimum of words.

'I think you'll see that it is,' I said, hoping against hope that I was right. 'The dog had rabbit fleas.'

Fraser was looking so bemused that I felt almost sorry for him. 'How in hell do you know a rabbit flea from any other sort of flea?' he demanded.

I gave thanks for Isobel's expertise. 'Rabbit fleas are black,' I told him. 'Cat fleas are brown. Ninety-eight per cent of fleas on dogs and cats are cat fleas but if a dog picks up a myxied rabbit the fleas take the opportunity to transfer onto a living host until they get a chance to get back onto a rabbit. Mrs Horner's cat has been boarded with us since the evening of the day she died and it had rabbit fleas when it came in. Mrs Kitts, my veterinarian partner, had examined the cat that morning and it was clear. That may not be enough to satisfy you that that dog and that cat came into contact on that day, but it'll do for me.

'So Bovis paid a call. Mrs Horner then dropped her bombshell. She had a fondness for Bovis but Bovis's wife had just left him for his partner, Mrs Horner's nephew, Ian Shute. Mrs Horner took Bovis's part against her own nephew and she told him that she was going to cut her nephew out of her will.

'This would have been disaster. The partnership is in need of money. Mrs Horner had nothing to leave but the house and contents, but there is an overlooked remnant of the family heirlooms in the dining room, a very valuable painting which Bovis has just described as comparatively worthless. If anybody should have known its value, he should. Another painting by the same artist sold recently for a quarter of a million. That sort of legacy to his partner would save both their bacons and it was about to slip out of reach.

'Thinking very quickly, he snatched her earring. At a guess, I'd suggest that he pretended to be swatting at a wasp. The earring went into the water butt and, when she peered or groped in after it, she followed it in.

'After the deed, he'd only have to set the scene — fetch the tongs from the house, position the box, exit by her back gate, collect the dog-crap and one of Mr Branch's cigar butts, put them in place, deposit a little ash on the dead woman's back and go home by the way he came.'

Fraser was frowning in thought. 'I was told that he was at an auction that day.'

'I'm afraid not. Inspector Blosson should have checked with the auctioneer. I've just been told that Bovis left his bids the day before.'

We had quite forgotten that Mrs Guidman was there. When she spoke softly, I think that we both jumped. 'He was hame a that day,' she said. 'When he taks oot his car, I aye hear the motor on his garage door. It maks an awfu noise on my wee radio.'

DS Parkes coughed discreetly. 'Mr Blosson saw Mr Bovis's receipt from the auctioneers, sir,' he said. 'He took that as enough confirmation of his alibi. Of course,' he added apologetically, 'he knew nothing of any motivation.'

'I think I want a word with Mr Bovis,' Fraser said. He left the room and after a second or two I followed, out of sheer, inexcusable nosiness.

'Where is he?' Fraser was asking Bruce.

'He went home to fetch something,' Bruce said. 'He'll be back.'

'He will, will he? Could he have heard what Mr Cunningham and I were saying to each other?'

'I suppose he could,' Bruce said slowly. 'He was looking at that tapestry picture just inside the door and then he went out into the hall. A minute or two later he put his head round the door and said that he wanted a reference book.'

Fraser said a word which is not supposed to pass the lips of a police officer on duty. 'Sergeant,' he then called loudly. 'Come.'

★   ★   ★

The two officers moved with surprising speed, gathering up Sergeant Morrison as they went. I almost managed to keep up with them but Bruce who, from some lawyerly instinct, had lingered to lock up the house, was left behind. Mrs Guidman, I learned later, was nearly locked in the house but caught Bruce's attention just in time.

Ahead of me, as I emerged, I saw Fraser try Bovis's side gate, find it bolted and move on round the corner into the village street.

The garden wall was too high to see over, but the front gates were lower and of wrought iron. Fraser paused in front of them, puffing slightly. 'You'd better be right,' he told me grimly as I caught up with him. 'We'll look a right bunch of gowks, arriving like a . . . a posse in the Wild West, if he really has only come to fetch the *Dealer's Guide to Commodes* or some such thing. The case against him's no less circumstantial than the case against Alistair Branch. Fleas, for God's sake!'

'And motivation,' I said, 'and trying to cloud the issue of where he was that day. And flight.'

'If he walks out of there — '

'With the *Dealer's Guide to Antique Chamber Pots* or some such reference work,' I said, 'you'll have your head in a sling. I know that. But it won't happen. He's guilty. I can feel it in my water.'

Fraser said something terrible about my water.

Bovis's exit was somewhat more dramatic than we had been envisaging. I heard the sound of an electric motor and then that of a starter. The garage door was going up and I saw that Bovis was already backing his car out of the garage. He had a remote control, because the heavy metal gates suddenly began to open. Fraser grasped them and the safety cut-out checked the motor. Bovis had turned the car on the gravel in front of the house and accelerated towards us. I could see him stabbing with his finger at what I took to be the remote control for the gates. The motor repeatedly started and checked but Sergeant Parkes, thinking quickly, had produced a pair of handcuffs from somewhere under his jacket and linked the two gates together. Even if Bovis rammed the gates, the impact would disable his car.

The car slid to a halt just short of the gates. Bovis slammed the car into reverse and spurted back up the short drive, looking over his shoulder and aiming for the garage doorway. There was the sound of metal-work crumpling and then the car was inside. The gates were only half the height of the wall and the three policemen hurdled them and ran, but the door was already descending and it shut with a clang before Fraser, the fleetest of the three, could get near. He turned and darted to the front door but it was securely locked and bolted. I followed on. I had entered with great reluctance into the investigation but now I was sharing in the thrill of the chase.

'You two,' Fraser gasped out. 'Round to the far corners. Watch the back and sides. But don't take any risks.' The two Sergeants vanished. Fraser sounded a long peal on the doorbell. He was beginning to recover his breath. 'Come out, Mr Bovis. We only want to talk to you.' No reply came from within. 'You've nowhere to go. The house is surrounded.' Which I suppose it was, after a fashion.

The centre of the garden was mostly taken up by a raised bed of flowers, meticulously tidy as in Mrs Horner's garden, but shrubs had been allowed to form jungle at either side, to provide the necessary facilities for an ageing dog I supposed. Blitzen, the old Airedale, roused himself and hobbled out of a clump of broom. He sniffed us both, decided that he had met me before and that Detective Superintendent Fraser was harmless, and lay down on a patch of lawn, awaiting events.

There was a bow window to our left. I only had to take a few paces sideways and I was looking in. I could see Bovis moving around in what seemed to be a well-furnished sitting room. His face was so distorted by conflicting emotions that I could have expected an attack of apoplexy at any moment but his movements were controlled. From glass cases and off the walls he was assembling a collection of weapons which would have done credit to a mediaeval fortress. While I watched, he placed a formidable battleaxe upright beside the door, drew a beautiful samurai sword from its sheath and made a few whistling passes in the air.

'Is that real?' Fraser asked softly beside me. He seemed to have accepted my presence as a sort of honorary member of the team.

'They used to test them on the bodies of criminals,' I said. 'They were expected to slice right through at one stroke. And that won't be a fake. He's an antique dealer, remember.'

Bovis saw me through the window and his face darkened further. He made a slash in my direction with the sword and, although I knew that there was glass between us, I stepped back involuntarily.

'That does it,' Fraser said. He pulled me by the arm towards the front door, out of Bovis's sight. 'He's gone round the bend. I've seen it before.'

Fraser had a small personal radio in his hand. He gave a code word and started speaking. He was asking for back-up and I could hardly blame him. If Bovis was preparing for a siege, it might well be a long one. There would be plenty of food and water in the house and it would be a brave officer who broke in to face a maddened man and that collection of weaponry.

I was not paying much attention to what Fraser was saying but was looking towards the small gathering of interested spectators at the gate, Bruce and Mrs Guidman among them. But when Fraser finished his call, his concluding words were still in my ears. 'For God's sake,' I said, 'you don't want an Armed Response Team.'

'Believe me,' Fraser said, 'I do. That man is armed. Take a look.'

I looked. Bovis was sitting with the samurai sword within reach. On the coffee table in front of him he had opened a neat wooden box with fitted compartments and he was using a small copper powder flask to load the cylinders of an elaborately engraved, mid-nineteenth-century Tranter revolver.

'I'm going to talk to him,' I said.

'For God's sake don't interfere. He has a revolver.'

'He hasn't had time to load it.' I said. 'I may be able to save you from having to fight a small war.'

'I can't forbid you to talk to a neighbour. Be quick, then,' Fraser said wearily. 'And watch out for yourself. There was a crossbow on the wall. And just be damn sure you don't get taken hostage.'

I rang the bell and, for good measure, rapped with a neat antique knocker of a satyr's head. 'Bovis,' I called. 'Come to the door. It's me, John Cunningham.'

My voice brought him to the other side of

the door before I was ready for him. 'You bastard!' he roared.

'I'm trying to help you,' I said.

'You've helped me enough already.' A faint, metallic sound at the letter box gave me a tenth of a second's warning and I jerked aside. A spear came through the letter box at waist height with great force, missing me by a centimetre. My instinct was to make several more backward leaps in case the next thing to emerge was a crossbow quarrel, but my earlier training and experience in hand-to-hand combat came back to me. Before he could recover his balance, I grasped the polished wooden shaft and pulled with a violence matching his. The spear came easily then checked. He must have hurt his fingers against the inside of the letter box because I heard a thud and a yelp. The spear came clear but in the process the shaft snapped. The metal tip was like a knife blade and it was sharp as a thorn. I dropped both halves on the ground.

Blitzen got to his feet and barked. His tail was thrashing, almost pulling him off his old feet.

'No!' Bovis's voice wailed. 'That was an original Zulu assegai.'

I forced down my rising temper and wiped a sudden sweat off my face. Fraser had joined me. We were standing with our backs to the wall beside the front door, out of Bovis's sight for the moment, but not if he made a sudden sortie or came to the bay window. At least, I decided, he was still thinking like an antique dealer. There was hope yet. 'Now you've got two of them,' I said. 'And if you try it again with that sword, I'll tie it in a knot. What the hell do you think you're playing at?'

'I'm not playing.'

'He's right,' Fraser said. 'He isn't playing. You have guns at home, don't you?'

'You know I do. And they're staying there,' I said.

'It could be an hour before armed officers get here. Suppose he makes a sortie, takes a hostage and another car?'

'I don't think his mind works that way. If I fetched my guns and he did break out, who would do the shooting, you or me?'

'I could authorize their use.'

'Thanks very much.' I could visualize myself being ordered to shoot and then having my firearms confiscated during the legal processes leading to a public inquiry and another round of legislation constricting the gun owner. The police do not have a good record of playing fair when it comes to firearms legislation.

Fraser was interrupted before he could

make any rash promises or produce more arguments. His personal radio made electronic noises at him. He answered impatiently. The sound reproduction was not very clear but I could make out the message. Backup, with armed officers, would be on the way shortly. And there was a longer message from Records. Blosson, when a constable, had been the subject of a complaint from Alistair Branch, supported by four other motorists, arising from an occasion when the officer had attempted to prosecute Alistair for speeding. He had made a formal statement that he had followed Alistair for more than a mile but the other motorists, who included a magistrate and a professor of Scots law, supported the complaint that the panda car had only come out of a side road a few yards before the derestriction sign. The incident, and the fuss that Blosson made while refusing to admit that he had erred, resulted in a black mark on his record which he only left behind by taking the Criminal Investigation course.

'Give it up,' Fraser said softly beside me. 'Come away. We'll bring in a trained negotiator.'

I nodded, but I rather resented his lack of faith in my powers of reasoning. I decided to have one more shot. I rapped on the door again, keeping well to one side.

Instead of coming to the door, Bovis suddenly slid up the lower sash of the window. He was still nursing the Tranter revolver. I could see the brass percussion caps on the nipples. He was only a few feet away and there was no longer the illusion of a protective glass pane between us. Fraser moved with amazing speed. One moment he was beside me, the next he had taken several quick strides and dived through the roses into safety behind the raised flower bed. It was too late for me to move. Fraser's flight would have prepared Bovis and he would be ready to take a snap shot at me. It is not easy to hit a moving target with a handgun, especially for a novice, but I was not going to take any chances on beginner's luck.

Bovis was glaring at me from the window. 'You betrayed me,' he said. The revolver was pointing somewhere in the vicinity of my navel. I could see the spherical balls in the chambers. So he had had the necessary components available.

I could have debated the question of betrayal, but he was in no mood for a discussion of semantics. I wished that I was grovelling in the grass beside Fraser but I was committed now. Sweet reason might be my only weapon. 'If you hadn't tried to frame it onto Alistair Branch,' I said, 'I'd never have become involved at all.'

Bovis may have been expecting apology or bluster. The intrusion of logic into our dialogue caught him unprepared. He frowned and then spoke more reasonably. 'He'd have been all right. They'd never have got a conviction on that evidence.' He sounded more calm, now that the effort of thinking was forced on him.

'And that made it all right?' I asked. 'He could have spent longer in the jug, waiting to come to trial, than he'd have served if he'd kicked somebody's teeth in.'

There was a long silence. He had lowered the revolver to his side. At least he was starting to think. If he was still capable of feeling guilt, there might be a chance. 'Where were you going to go?' I asked.

'I'd have found somewhere.'

'I doubt it. What do you hope to gain by fighting off the whole police force now? They'd be watching for you to pop up in the world of antiques. Do you intend to make a fresh career in crime? Or will you look for work as a labourer?'

There was another long pause. 'Once I've given up,' he said, 'it's over.'

With a slight sense of guilt I found that I could almost sympathize with his view. Once he was in custody, he would be a prisoner, a number, a man with a huge gap in his future. Until then, he could hope for a miracle, an inspiration, a thunderbolt, a *deus ex machina*, something, anything, to keep putting off the moment of arrest. He was in much the same position as the man who fell off the tall building; as he passed the second floor he was heard to say, 'So far so good!'

'I'll stick it out,' he said. 'I'll hold out as long as I can. Then . . . '

'You'll do something stupid?' It was the universal euphemism for suicide.

'Not so stupid. Better than the other thing.' He had raised the revolver again, this time laying it on his shoulder and almost against his ear.

'You're only making it worse for yourself.'

'How?'

Once again, he had a point. In the long term, not much could be added to a life sentence and there has never been a convincing deterrent to suicide. I have no moral objection to suicide and I would certainly have preferred that he shot himself rather than me, but on the whole it seemed that it would be a wrong but irreversible action taken in the haste of the moment. I groped for an idea. Bovis had not given a damn when his wife left him but there was one being he still cared for.

'Don't you mind what happens to Blitzen?' I asked.

'What do you mean?' he asked sharply. 'What about him?'

I was not quite sure what I meant but I had gained his full attention. I was speaking before I had quite thought out what I was going to say. 'Blitzen will go into the police pound. He'll miss you. He'll get a poor diet, minimal care and no companionship. He'll die of a broken heart. He'll be sure that you abandoned him in his old age.'

Recognizing his name, Blitzen came over and leaned against my leg. 'Blitzen likes you,' he said wonderingly. 'If I give up now, you'll keep him for me? Is that what you mean?'

The last thing that I wanted was an ageing free-loader in need of regular care, but I had talked myself into it. 'Come out now without further trouble,' I said, 'and I'll look after Blitzen as long as he lives. Or until you can look after him again yourself.'

'Word of honour?'

'Word of honour.'

The schoolboy phrase seemed to reassure him. There was another long silence. The crowd at the gate had swollen. They were listening avidly.

'All right,' Bovis said suddenly. 'Tell them to cool it. I'm coming out.'

★ ★ ★

It was all over bar the shouting, most of which took place in court. When Roland Bovis was brought to trial in Dundee, I was not required as a witness. I was too busy to spend whole days in the courtroom but the trial was fully reported in the *Courier* and elsewhere.

The shouting, or at least the haranguing in a booming voice that rattled the windows, was mostly the work of the advocate for the defence. He poured scorn on the circumstantial evidence. Isobel, who landed the job of giving the evidence about fleas, came in for her share but I heard that she stood her ground. It was the forensic scientific evidence which counted most heavily against him. In particular, the water butt had overflowed on Mrs Horner's enforced entry, wetting Bovis's shoes with water tainted by the weed-killer, fertilizer, foliar feed and several insecticides that she habitually used. The combination turned out to be unique and traces were found on his shoes and the cuffs of a pair of trousers. The jury took several hours to arrive at a verdict but in the end he was convicted.

I still cannot work up a dislike of Bovis although I know that his crime was a savage act committed for purely selfish motives and that, through my own rashness, I came very near to death at his hands. There are those in the village who feel that Mrs Horner should have been drowned at birth and that anyone caring to remedy the omission at a later date could not be all bad. I do know that he receives regular parcels of comforts from a group of supporters and his house is kept repaired and tenanted, ready for his return some day in the still rather remote future.

I am left with one genuine regret. Blitzen was not with us for long. He did not die of a broken heart. He was being walked by one of the juniors alongside the road when he jerked his lead out of the unready hand in order to chase a cat across the road in front of an approaching van. The cat made it. Blitzen, being old and stiff, did not. It could be argued that I had kept my promise to Bovis, but I still feel guilty. That is why I sometimes make a contribution towards the food parcels.

Detective Inspector Blosson took early retirement on health grounds rather than face a disciplinary hearing over an investigation carried out sloppily and with bias. He is now in Aberdeen and working for ex-Inspector Burrard who, I understand, keeps him firmly in line.